"At once futuristic and nostalgic, *Arrokoth* is reminiscent of Malerman's *Inspection* with its edgy, coming of age dynamics. Engaging, soul searching, and dare I say, a prescient looksee at the near future?"

— Justin Holley, author of *Seven Cleopatra Hill* and *Hellweg's Keep*

"*Arrokoth* is a brilliant novella, deeply human and mind-teasing. Mia Dalia is a fabulous writer, managing to offer us a jewel of both dark and light beauty and a perfect parable on human nature. An absolute must-read for lovers of humanist sci-fi!"

— Seb Doubinsky, the author of *City-States* series

"I couldn't put it down. A story of hope, betrayal, and love with the intensity only science fiction can deliver. Arrayed against a life-and-death science fiction struggle, this is a story about abiding hope and love."

— Sue Burke, author of *Semiosis* duology & *Dual Memory*

"Mia Dalia offers a tale that offers the best of what science fiction is and should be. A believable world, filled with technical and scientific wonders and terrors, and an artful examination of the human condition and the human heart—even when it seems like the story relates to the mind. You'll see…"

—Jeffrey Caston, author of *Immunity*

"An eloquent and moving tale of deep space and inner conflicts where human advancement clashes with the cycles of history, *Arrokoth* is both a voyage through space that explores the intellectual curiosity and simple pleasures of being human and a touching portrayal of a superior intelligence striving to advance civilization while confronting the harrowing truths of settling a new society. Dalia's crisp, compelling prose weaves together two distinct voices to create a layered observation about the range of human intelligence and the common ties that bind us."

— Brian Pinkerton, author of *The Gemini Experiment* and *The Intruders.*

Also by Mia Dalia

Estate Sale

Smile So Red

The Trunk

Spindel

Tell Me a Story

Discordant

ARROKOTH

MIA DALIA

Denver, Colorado

Published in the United States by:
Spaceboy Books LLC
1627 Vine Street
Denver, CO 80206
www.readspaceboy.com

ISBN: 978-1-951393-34-2
First printed June 2024

To Chelsea,
the brightest star in my sky.

DARYL

You're never too old to learn something new. I'm standing in the back of the auditorium, leaning against the wall. Trying to absorb the lecture.

I'm failing. I've done this before, numerous times, this auditing of the classes. The professors know about it. They are amused by it, I think.

I am not an ambitious man, I'm happy enough with my lot in life—I don't need to unlock the mysteries of the universe. The reason I'm here now, the reason I've come here before, is that my son is one of the kids in these seats, one of the kids to whom all the words the professor is saying make perfect sense. And I want to be part of that world, in whatever way I can.

When the lecture ends, I sneak away before the kids, pick up my mop and my bucket, and get back to work. Knowledge is grand and all that, but someone's got to keep this place clean. I make sure my son doesn't notice I was ever there.

Daryl and I are growing apart. I know it, I can feel it. How can we not? He is, after all, so much smarter than me. Smarter than most people. He's not the only one like that, every kid here at the Lyceum is a genius. I'm not exaggerating, I mean a literal, certifiable genius. The professors are barely keeping up with their learning demands. It's a strange new world, and the Lyceum was built specifically for it.

"Why not just call it school?" I asked Daryl one day.

"Because, Dad, school comes from the Greek word "*scholē*" which means leisure, and there's nothing leisurely about our studies."

The kid was six at the time.

He's twelve now. His IQ measures well above 200, and his interests and hobbies go right over my head. He no longer humors me by joining in to watch my favorite TV shows. I know they are simply not interesting enough for him, the way kids' cartoons wouldn't interest me. One day Daryl's going to invent something that'll change the world. Maybe even save it.

If there was ever a world in need of saving, we're on it. The West Coast is on fire, the East Coast is slowly drifting underwater. Florida's all but gone with Louisiana set to follow suit. People have been steadily moving toward the middle of the country and learning to survive the increasingly more dangerous tornadoes, preferring them to hurricanes. It's a world of choosing the lesser evil. The politicians lie. The pundits spin. Nothing gets solved, nothing gets fixed. In this world, I think my son and kids like him are our only hope. I've told him this and, having seen the *Star Wars* movies with me when he was younger, he was amused by the quote. But I don't know what he thinks of all this, and some days I'm afraid to ask. If things seem that bleak to an average guy like me, what must it be like for someone like my boy?

Our name is the only thing we share. I was named after a TV show character, my parents' favorite, a show about a very different kind of apocalypse from the one we're facing. And Sandy, my wife, thought it was as good of a name as any to pass on to our kid. Daryl Junior. DJ for the first few years, before he told us in no uncertain terms that he dislikes diminutives and doesn't see the purpose of such abbreviations. After all, no one was calling me DS for Daryl Senior. From then on, he was just Daryl, and I was just Dad. As I got older, I became Mr. Olsen at work. Mister being not so much a term of respect as a reflection of my age. It doesn't matter, though, so long as I get to be near my boy.

The Lyceum is a live-in school. The kids stay at the dormitories, it's meant to provide a less disruptive, less distracting environment for them. Daryl was right: there is indeed almost no leisure, though there are sports. Not sports as we think of them like chasing balls and scoring goals. These are more along the lines of strength and agility-building exercises. The kids run, swim, things like that. Apparently, it releases the right chemicals in their brains to stimulate learning and growth. I can't remember the names of the chemicals. Should have written them down.

Most of the time I don't write things down because there's no point to it. I know the gist of things, so I can do without the specifics. I don't need to know the exact portions of the grey matter that are hyperactive in Daryl and kids like him, they are just geniuses and that's that. They can absorb and process information in the way we, mere mortals, can only dream about. These kids make Einstein look average. In fact, there was an experiment not too long ago when one of these kids, the Chosen, as they are known colloquially, raised in isolation came up with a theory of relativity all on his own by the age of ten. Boggles the mind, doesn't it?

But here's what I do know, some facts. Sometime in the '50s, the scientists discovered thalidomide and thought it would be good to give to women to help them with pregnancy nausea. Soon enough, deformed babies were being born. Some didn't survive much longer past birth, some lived but with a variety of mutations. Good intentions—terrible results. Classic science fail.

Time passed, and history repeated itself. Scientists thought they finally figured it out. Their new wonder chemical combo, Amartium, took care of all major pregnancy discomforts, and people, with their short memories, flocked to it. The result was the same: deaths and mutations. Unlike the last time around, science tried to mess with nature in more elaborate ways: in babies that survived the mutations were solely in the brain. The babies born to women on Amartium were, well, geniuses.

It took a while to notice and even longer to address. With the long-term effects being uncertain, Amartium was immediately discontinued, but there were still thousands of kids out there with off-the-charts IQs. Kids who, by early age, spoke multiple languages, read at the college level, did complicated math, etc. They became known as the Chosen. The moniker might have started off as insulting or ironic, but it sure stuck, permanently enshrined in the popular vocabulary and used by everyone, albeit with a different inflection.

Since Amartium was produced by a US company and marketed almost exclusively to first-world countries, most of the kids were American. Only about a quarter of them were from other countries, mostly European and English speaking, hence the Lyceum being built in the States. This sparked all sort of restless chatter, but in the end, the race or nationality of the kids never really entered the conversation. It was just one of those things. Important enough to rise above all the noise.

There was other chatter, of course. You can't just have such a thing occur in silence. Social media blew up with details, memes, conspiracies. There was a lot of general ugliness.

Some of it cost me my marriage.

The women who bore these baby geniuses so different from the rest were treated with a strange sort of resentful reverence. They'd call them Mary, like they were bringing the new messiahs into the world, but it was a derogatory nickname. One that got spat rather than said.

My wife didn't appreciate the infamy, couldn't cope with the scorn, the jealousy concealed as interest. She was religious, and the "Mary" business sure enough seemed like a sacrilege to her. She left us when Daryl was just eight. By then, the kid was already a budding astronomer, already smarter than the two of us put together ever were.

"It isn't natural," she'd whisper to me in bed at night. "It's an aberration of nature. No one should be that smart. He won't even cuddle with me anymore. He's always lost in his books. He says things I can't understand, and I'm the adult here. It scares me."

I'd do my best to reassure her, tell her we don't know all the paths the evolution is meant to take. But after a while, there was no reassuring her. She left to join a commune, which, like so many communes, turned out to be a cult. Not the good kind. Not that there are any. I mean, I don't know the statistics, but I do know that after a while, they forbade her from communicating with us, allegedly so that "her soul could heal." Not sure if her soul was healed by the time she died there with all of them in a fire—a fire no one had ever conclusively determined as deliberate or unintentional. Maybe the building had faulty wiring. Maybe the people did. Either way, she was gone.

I grieved as much as it was possible to grieve for someone who had left you long before they had actually died. Daryl seemed fine, though. His approach to death, like so many things, was primarily analytical. I didn't have to help him cope with his mother's death and that was, in a way, the saddest thing of all.

To be close to the son who didn't seem to need me at all, or maybe just for myself, I got a janitorial job at the Lyceum. They call it something else to make the job sound fancier than it is, but it doesn't change my daily chores. I'm happy to be here, near my kid. I'm trying to learn something so that on those rare occasions we spend time together, he can feel like he can talk to me about the things that interest him. The Lyceum has given me a small cottage on the grounds to live in. I like it. Daryl visits me there from time to time, I've even learned to cook according to his dietary requirements. About the only fun thing we do together is watch the old show after which we were both named. It's violent and gory and potentially inappropriate for a kid, but Daryl's no ordinary kid.

He enjoys pointing out the logistical flaws in the story, but at least he seems entertained by it.

The Lyceum doesn't have a traditional grade system. The kids get a more individualized sort of education tailored to their specific fields of interest. With Daryl, it has always been space. He looks up at the night sky and dreams of things I can't even imagine.

When I ask him, he tells me, "Arrokoth."

"What's that?"

"An object at the farthest reaches of the known world," he explains. "In the past, it was sometimes understood to be a reference to an island far north of Britain considered the northernmost place explored by ancient humans. Then they named The Kuiper Belt object formerly known as 2014 MU69 Ultima Thule. Then they realized it had Nazi connotations—the Nazis referred to it as the mythical homeland of the Aryan people—so it was renamed once more as Arrokoth."

That's how my kid talks, just like a book, smarter than any book.

"What kind of name is Arrokoth?" I ask, trying to keep up.

"It means *sky* in the Powhatan and Algonquian languages."

"Oh," I respond. "OK then, interesting."

"We can discuss the way the political correctness of the early 20th century informed and colored the public discourse and nomenclature," Daryl suggests.

And then he smiles just enough to show me that this is still my kid, not a walking talking encyclopedia, still a good kid with a subtle but present sense of humor and something like affection for his old man.

"Why don't we have some ice cream instead," I say. It's a special kind, low in all the delicious things and with nothing artificial in it, but it's still a treat within the restrictive parameters of Lyceum's diet. "I won't tell if you don't."

"Deal," says Daryl mock solemnly and follows me back in.

It is only much later that night when I'm lying awake at night, waiting for sleep to take mercy on me, and Daryl's long gone back to the Lyceum, that it occurs to me I never really asked what is it about Arrokoth that so occupies his thoughts.

The later years in the Lyceum are more along the lines of guided studies. By then, the pupils have advanced way beyond their teachers. There's no set graduation date, either. The studies are finished when it is determined they are—a purely unique approach, custom-tailored to each pupil individually. Afterward, it is time for specialization.

I would have loved a proper graduation ceremony. Would have worn my only suit, old and dated, but still a good fit. Would have appreciated the ritual. But alas, everything about my son, everything about kids like him, is so far outside the dated traditions and normal social standards.

When he explains to me his perspective on things —sometimes, it sends shivers down my spine. It's so methodical, so logical, so … unfeeling. My boy is like Mr. Spock, another old TV show reference, without the funny ears and a funnier haircut.

And sure enough, when I try to understand him, when I try thinking as he does, so many conventions suddenly seem unnecessary. I wonder what sort of life it'll be for him, a life of a mind. I hope there'll be more to his life than his studies, but I believe that either way he will be happy, whatever his version of happiness might be.

There are things we still celebrate, like his birthdays. Once I even got it perfectly right: the year his mother left, I gave him a telescope. Not a cheapo kid's toy either, but a proper, expensive one. He figured out how to set it up almost immediately and spent hours that day as the evening turned to night in our backyard watching the skies. I'll never forget the look in his eyes when he came in. The kid was positively beaming.

"What'd you see?" I asked him.

"Everything," he answered dreamily. 'The past, the future."

"A lot of stars out there."

"Only about five thousand stars can be seen with a naked eye. The amount increases dramatically when a telescope is introduced. Depending on the lenses used, it can be a hundred thousand or even millions."

"Ah… any favorites?"

My son looked at me like I just asked him a ridiculous question. He often did, even back then, but he smiled anyway, in too good of a mood to be put off by his silly old dad.

"One day I'm going to discover a new one, and that'll be my favorite", he said matter-of-factly.

"A new star?"

"A new planet."

DAR

I never liked my name. I was named after my father who was named after an old TV character. Not the most auspicious of beginnings, not the most auspicious of monikers. Both men, the fictional and the real one, are perfectly good, decent, loyal, honest men. Neither are especially intelligent. And intelligence matters. It matters a great deal. For me and others like me, it may be the only thing that does.

But then again, this was never a perfect design. We, unimaginatively labeled the Chosen, were a snafu, a mistake, a random unintended mutation. Our IQs—our superpowers as it were—were a freak of a chemical reaction, not something genetically inherited and nurtured.

Is it still a gift? We used it as such, but this isn't a flawless system. So many Amartium kids came into the world stillborn, so many took their own lives later on when the onus of intellectual omnipotence proved to be too much, so many became addicts to cope with their differences or learned to hide their intellects to fit in with the normis. These brains of ours ... they are not an easy gift to live with. It's been argued they are not a gift at all. I disagree.

Here, at the Lyceum, we are the best of the best. The crème de la crème. The ones who survived, the ones who blossomed, the ones who persevered. We are the smartest people on Earth. We are reminded of this every day. We are the future.

Because I never liked my name and because as a child I had abysmal penmanship, the first three letters were often the only ones legible. Thus, I became Dar. I liked it much more. It was succinct and interesting sounding. It was years later that Corinne told me it meant *"a gift"* in Russian. Was I ever? For the longest time I was arrogant enough to think so. I thought all of us at the Lyceum were the greatest gift to humanity. I am no longer so sure. But then, certainty is a thing of youth. Now that I've had all this time to reflect, the nuances make themselves more and more apparent. And I wonder ....

Here on this ship, we are encouraged to keep logs. But the daily goings-on of a perfectly automated fine-tuned system aren't interesting enough in and of themselves, and it leaves time, so much time, for idle contemplation. I have decided to set some of my thoughts down for posterity. Whether they prove to be inspirational, instructional, or cautionary I cannot say. But it has been said that the unexamined life isn't worth living, and so, I examine mine. I only hope I shall like what I discover.

My early years were marked by the unflagging devotion of my father and the conflicting, troubled love of my mother. The latter was a weak individual, possibly unsuited to motherhood altogether, and certainly unsuited to mothering of an exceptional child. I am told I showed the signs of being exceptional early enough. By the time the official test results came in, my mother was already deeply in the throes of her faulty ideologies. She left us, and then she died. I know I should care more about this, but she was never a loving presence in my life, all too soon becoming no more than a ghost. I don't think I ever missed her. I don't think I ever loved her.

It is important to point out here that we the Chosen have been known to struggle with concepts like love. I can sooner explain quantum physics to you than the mechanics of the human heart. We deal with tangible, quantifiable matters. Feelings ... feelings are difficult.

My dad was easier to care about, an easy man to know. Profoundly uncomplicated and genuinely caring, he always, *always* made every effort to understand his unfathomable son. I remember seeing him at the back of the auditorium, auditing the classes I was taking. He thought he blended right into the shadows, and I never corrected him, but it was ... touching. That a man like that, with only a high-school education, would try to follow the Chosen's curriculum just to have something to talk to his son about.

He also gave me my first glimpse of the stars. My best birthday present for years was a telescope. It wasn't anywhere near modern standards, not since one of us has redesigned high-resolution telescope lenses that revolutionized how much of the skies we can see and know, but it was surprisingly good for the time. It must have cost him a pretty penny, not that he's ever mentioned it.

From a financial perspective, having a kid like me was easy as pie. Actually, I don't get that simile, there's nothing easy about making a pie, but that's what people say. Maybe they mean eating a pie, but I digress.

The government paid for everything for us: gave my father a job, a small house, gave me a place to live, to study, to excel. I never had to worry about a single thing outside of studying and reaching my full potential. If you love studying as much as I did—as much as I *do*—it's a great and easy life.

So, the telescope … yes. It was like being given a ticket to the greatest show outside of Earth. My father thought it would cheer me up and distract me from my mother's leaving, but unlike him, I was neither sad nor distraught about it. It didn't matter. And soon, nothing mattered outside of those glittering celestial promises above me.

I knew what my focus would be then. In normi universities, they call them "*majors*." In Lyceum they call them "*foci*." I don't like the word *focuses*, though it is also acceptable in American English. I always found American English to be the laziest of all versions, and Corinne concurs. Or maybe I got the idea from Corinne and learned to see the truth of it. Anyway, I knew I was to be an astronomer.

For years it was all I thought of. The stars above me were the most beautiful thing I ever saw. Until I met Corinne.

That didn't happen until later. She came to the Lyceum when we were both twelve. Until then, her parents had tried to deny how exceptional their daughter was by hiding her away among the normis in a Belgian village of Dinant, known as the birthplace of the man who invented the saxophone and not much else. Eventually, they gave in to the inevitable, and there she was, a coltish preteen, all knees and elbows and a funny accent. She fell in with our circle easily enough, she was just as serious, just as determined as any of us, perhaps more so for all the catching up she had to do. We became friends easily enough, both belonging to the same clique, though these cliques were never exclusive or set in stone, more of amorphous conglomerates based on shared interests and fields of study. She soon declared her focus to be linguistics. By the time I fell in love with her, she had mastered seven languages. At the time of my writing this, that number stood at twenty-nine.

A genius. Of course. Just like the rest of us.

What else can I tell you about my time at the Lyceum?

I suppose I must mention Zilla. It is, after all, one of the main reasons we are all here on this ship. Zilla is my best friend, if I was to give myself over to cheap sentimentality. My confidante. The smartest person I ever met. That last one, that says a lot, doesn't it? All I knew were smart people, and Zilla stood out among them proudly and prominently. Zilla was always going to change the world, we just never knew how. His foci kept changing. He couldn't sit still, as if he was too excited for too many things. At times, it seemed he was destined to become a talented dilettante, someone with surface knowledge (thought the Chosen one's surface knowledge is still quite vast) of a great many things, but a master of none.

For the longest time, I didn't even know his real name. It must have been something too plain, too unoriginal, like mine. Many of us changed our names at the Lyceum. We were all about self-determination in every way possible. Zilla said his name was an atheist version of his favorite monster. It was all very "on-brand" for him—Zilla was always obsessed with retro media. There was no old movie, no vintage science fiction paperback, no bygone superhero that Zilla didn't know and love *and* quote from, extensively. I used to think he'd specialize in media studies, but then, of course, he went and reinvented space travel.

Zilla and I met in our first year at the Lyceum and shared a Hab since. Hab is short for "*habitation*" not a misspelling of hub. Our space was designed by people with a fine appreciation of ancient times and languages. They were also minimalists, specializing in well-lit, modest spaces just comfortable enough to make you feel at ease but not enough to encourage too much idle lounging. For we The Chosen had busy, busy lives and much to get done.

Around the time Zilla was fourteen, he became obsessed with antimatter. It dominated our conversations.

It wasn't enough for me to find a new planet, Zilla wanted to make sure we can go there. He studied every method, from the solar sails to nuclear fusion reactors. He even mulled over the old science fiction plots in his mind. But what he always came back to was antimatter.

"It's the only way, Dar," he'd say.

"It's impossibly, prohibitively expensive," I'd counter, comfortable in my role as devil's advocate.

"Not if we harvest it directly from Van Allen's belt where it occurs naturally."

"It's impossible to store."

"Penning Trap."

"A Penning Trap cannot contain uncharged particles."

"That's what the atomic traps are for. You perfect a Penning trap by combining it with an atomic trap and maximize storage of the final product."

"You make it sound easy."

"It won't be, but it doesn't matter so long as it can be done."

"And then what? Use it as fuel?"

"No, no, absolutely not, that would never work. It's too dense, way denser than conventional fuel, the spacecraft would have to have a much higher thrust-to-weight ratio. And the idea is to make it lighter."

"So then what?"

"Smashy smash." He laughed, slapping his hands together in a deafening clap. "Collide matter with antimatter, and the released energy will propel you right to the stars."

"That simple?"

"Nothing simple about it, Jimmy. You gotta make sure your electron/positron reactions and their byproducts cooperate, sort out your pions."

"Pions?" It rang a bell, but was far enough outside of my focus to merit a refresher.

"Yeah, the neutral ones will vamoose on you almost immediately. You need to harvest the charged ones, and you need to direct their thrust magnetically in the right direction."

"Aha, pions."

"Quirky little quirks." Zilla smirked. "Eventually, charged pions will turn to neutrinos and unstable charged muons, the latter will then become a combo of neutrinos, electrons, and positrons, and those final neutrinos can carry about 2/3 of the muons' energy."

"So, you can more or less calculate the final output," I extrapolated.

"Something like that. It's all there, the science is there. It just needs to be finetuned."

"One more thing."

"Yes?"

"Who's Jimmy?"

"Jimmy Olsen. One of the all-time sidekick greats. Hung around Superman and his Clark Kent persona."

"Right. Nice. And this is because we're both Olsens, or because you think of yourself as Superman?"

"Oh, come on, man. We are all Supermen and Superwomen here at the Lyceum, aren't we? It's kind of our thing."

He was right, of course. And like proper superheroes, we wanted to fly. And so, we did. Zilla finetuned his ideas just as he envisioned and propelled us to the stars. I am floating among them now.

DARYL

I never dreamt of the stars. When I was younger, all of my dreams were much more pedestrian, much more practical. I dreamt of owning a sports car. Going on dates with beautiful girls. I never gave too much thought to the future, my immediate present was always enough. In retrospect, that's no way to live, because look at me now—I'm a guy pushing a mop around kids smarter than me in every possible way; my livelihood and my home are both provided solely due to my exceptional son. I get it, I get it. I know my place.

I was never voted most likely to succeed in high school, but I was reasonably popular. I was tall, I was fun, I knew my way around a basketball and a guitar. Friends and girls came easily to me. Learning didn't, but I managed to pass all the grades. I was invited to every party back then. At one of those parties, I met Annie.

We knew each other from around, but never really spoke until that night. She was a goody two-shoes preacher's daughter in the early throes of the downward spiral of her rebellion, having only recently discovered booze, pot, and other teen-favorite recreational activities. I was all too happy to help. She was pretty, not beautiful, not in the timeless classic way real beauty presents itself, but in the less permanent, more fleeting variety of radiant, glowing youth; a sunny strawberry blonde who snuck out party clothes in her backpack and changed outside of her house.

We didn't plan what happened next. Turned out neither of us was much into planning. Her pregnancy was a surprise to both of us, but not a shock. The shock came in learning she wanted to keep it. For all her newly acquired rebel ways, Annie was still a preacher's daughter, the ingrained ideology impossible to shake. Life was sacred to Annie, unplanned or otherwise, and so we geared up to be parents. I did the honorable thing, bought a ring, asked the question. We got married, her father glaring at me the entire time. My parents, day-drinking, resigned.

I didn't even have any college plans to abandon, so I got a job. Just one of the many meaningless manual labor jobs I've had until this one. Enough to provide for my new family, just barely, but no fun extras. I traded in my lovingly restored '67 Mustang for a more sensible four-door sedan. That one stung, but alas, those were the costs of adulthood.

I couldn't tell you if I ever really loved Annie the way they write about in books. I'm not sure she ever loved me that way. But there was something like warm affection between us for a while, and we both loved our kid. A perfect bouncing baby boy. The heir inheritor to the Olsens' nonexistent fortune.

Whatever fortune there was came from Annie's side of the family. The sight of baby Daryl Jr. melted her father's heart just enough for him to occasionally help us out financially. Eventually, he even paid for Annie to go get a degree. She made it through about a year and a half of community college before quitting. Apparently, higher education did not agree with her, though that year and a half entitled her for the rest of her days to say that she went to college.

I was never quite sure as to what she did with her days, what she loved to do. She enjoyed being with Daryl Jr., but as his differences became too glaring to ignore, and the battery of tests commenced, she drifted further and further from him, from us. There was something about her that loved a small, neatly organized life, a well contained and ordered world, and our modest home was always a testament to it: not a thing out of place. Even I fit it into this idea of hers well enough. But when it became obvious that her son was meant for a world and a life so much larger and more complicated than that, it did something to her. It pulled her forcibly in a direction she didn't want to take, and she rebounded like a rubber band, snapping shut, retreating into herself. Withdrawing into her religious ways more and more. Seeking comfort in the familiar and known.

Funnily enough, I was intrigued by all this Chosen business, pleased, delighted, exhilarated even, to have such an extraordinary son. I've never been around anyone that smart until now. Most people I knew were much like me, thoroughly and unremarkably average. But this kid, the things he said, the things he thought, the toppling piles of books around his room ... it was the wildest thing.

I tried to be a good dad. Always. I may not have been the best provider or the best husband, but no one can fault me as a dad. My kid's the greatest thing that has ever happened to me. Maybe even to the world at large.

Earth doesn't have a lot of time left. Everyone knows it. A few decades ago, there were warnings. We hit the turning point, the scientists said. If we don't change our ways dramatically and immediately, this is it, the experts proselytized. And did people listen?

No, they didn't. Or not enough of them did, anyway. Because at the end of the day, everyone still wanted what they wanted when they wanted it and wasn't willing to make any sacrifices in the present for the future they refused to give proper credence to.

Now, our planet is spiraling the drain of the devastating effects of climate change, and it's only a matter of time until it sinks all the way down. The future lies elsewhere. Quite possibly on the distant world my son has discovered.

DAR

Much has been written about memory. The way we reinvent a thing every time we recollect it. The inconstancy and inconsistency of it. And no matter how advanced our brains may be, we are all susceptible to those biases. I know because every time I go to narrate this blog, it takes me to strange and different places. Out of order. Out of time.

And so, I surrender. I will be a willing participant in this experiment of mine. I'll go where the memories take me. If nothing else, it'll pass the time.

We had a team of psychologists at the Lyceum, always on hand to help us navigate the world, specifically the world outside school—the unpredictable real world. A certain number of regular sessions was mandatory, but outside of that, it was on an as needed basis.

I don't recall ever wanting to talk to any of them. Feelings weren't that interesting of a topic for me. It's a thing with all of us, the Chosen. The unquantifiable, vague, and tenuous feelings tend to take the back seat to the quantifiable, knowable, provable facts. Reason and rationale rule. Mr. Spock was a sentimental softie in comparison to most of us.

Corinne was the only thing that threw me. The way I got tongue-tied in her presence. The way my heart rate accelerated.

I tried talking about it to my dad, but it was too awkward. I didn't think he had much experience in the romance department. His marriage was, objectively, a disaster, though my existence makes it impossible to call it a failure. He seldom dated. I wanted facts, data, statistics. And so, I went and spoke with one of the psychologists. They encouraged informality in those offices.

"Dan, call me Dan" wore jeans and a button-down with the top button open. His glasses had thick stylish frames. He was hip, as far as I could tell anyway.

"So, what do you want to talk about today—" He consulted his screen. "—Daryl?"

"Dar," I automatically corrected him. I was Dar to everyone by then, though no one was to call me that in front of my dad. I thought it would upset him. To this day, I don't know if he ever picked up on the naming duality.

"Dar then." Dan smiled. "What's up?"

"There's a new girl ..." I started.

"Sounds promising." He nodded, maintaining a smile.

"I think I love her."

"I see. Does she love you?"

"I don't know. I never asked. Should I ask?"

"Well, let's back up for a moment. This girl ... how well do you know her?"

"We're friends. She's one of my best friends. We share some interests."

"And do you have a reason to believe she might want to be more than friends?"

"I don't know. What would that reason present itself as?"

"Does she want to spend time with you and you alone? Does she display any body language that might suggest her attraction to you? Does she show more interest in you than her other friends? More than your other friends?"

"That's a lot." I paused, chewing my lip in thought.

"I know it is," Dan agreed, amiably. "Feelings are complicated and messy."

"I would prefer not to feel them."

"Impossible, my friend, I'm afraid. I don't care how smart you are. It's just one of those life things."

"It seems unreasonable."

"People say it's worth it."

"Poets?"

"Everyone, really."

"So, what is your practical advice? I should somehow assess her feelings without revealing mine and hope that we are copasetic on this matter?"

"Something like that."

"I don't like it," I said. "I appreciate your time and your thoughts, but I don't think it'll work for me."

"What will you do instead?"

"I'll figure something out," I told him with a surprising amount of confidence and shook his hand.

Next week during our otium, a time set aside for leisure and contemplation, I approached Corinne as she dozed with a book under her favorite tree.

"Wittgenstein," I noted, nodding to her book cover. She was one of the only people I knew who still read paper.

She blinked, her sleep so light as to vanish instantly at a single word.

"Oh hi, Dar," she said. "Yes, I'm thinking of taking on his ideas on solipsism in language for my next term paper."

"That's very interesting," I said genuinely.

"What are you up to?"

"I wanted to talk to you."

"Sounds serious." She smiled. Her accent came out on the second word.

"I wanted to tell you I love you."

She burst into a laugh, then covered her face. I didn't know what to make of that reaction. She took her hands away, and I saw a smile.

"You love me?"

"I do. Its incontrovertible."

"And what are you going to do about it?" When Corinne smiled like that, she made me feel younger, less mature. We were the same age, but she has lived in the outside world with the normis for much longer. There was a certain wealth of experience that came with that, something I wasn't privy to.

"Nothing as of now, I think. I will wait for you to reciprocate my feelings. This changes nothing, it was just something I wanted you to know. About the future. About *our* future."

"I thought your future was in the stars."

"*Our* future is in the stars, Corinne," I corrected her. "You'll see."

To this day I don't know where that pure confidence came from, it was... outside of reason. And nothing changed between us, not for a long time, but the seed was planted.

It stands to mention now, that confidence came in pretty handy later in life.

Like many of the Chosen, I was obsessed with the future. It held endless possibilities while the present offered nothing but constant disappointment. We came along too late for any actionable change here on Earth. It was time to cast our gaze to the stars.

I knew from an early age there was more out there than we knew about, more even than most dreamt about. The odds of there not being a suitable planet, something that meets the Goldilocks presets, something that might be hospitable to our species, in all of the cosmos were infinitesimal. I knew what to look for, I just had to know where to look.

I never stopped peering through telescopes. But I also took the scientific approach, burying myself in calculations. In 1846, Le Verrier predicted the existence and location of Neptune using only mathematics. Celestial mechanics were validated once and for all. I was determined to follow in his footsteps.

"It might just be another Vulcan you're hunting down," Zilla would tell me, referring to the ghost planet erroneously hunted down by Le Verrier following his success with Neptune. Le Verrier figured it was spinning somewhere between Mercury and the Sun. He was wrong.

"I have a genius IQ and the twenty-first-century math and tech. I should be able to dance the proverbial circles around Le Verrier's ideas and methods."

"And what will you name it when you find it? Which ancient deity will get the honor?"

"Well, thinking of Arrokoth, named and re-named, I suppose I should probably avoid naming it after anything known."

"You might be right," piped in Ton, the perpetually stoned cultural anthropologist and historian among us. "Avoid any potential negative connotations, etc." He made a disapproving face at odds with his normally mellow features.

Ton, a longtime friend, was remarkably high functional for a stoner. He said it was the only way he could slow down his brain to manageable speeds. He grew his own in a terrific small hydroponic setup in his walk-in closet, something he put together with Alice, a green-thumbed Aussie transplant with a focus on sustainable agriculture.

"I think the age of rampant and contextless political correctness might be waning," said Zilla. "Take your Arrokoth, for instance. In theory, Ultima Thule historically predates any Aryan associations."

"So does the swastika, but you don't see that used anywhere. No one's even used the name Adolf in what? A century or more?"

"That's actually an interesting note," said Ton, sitting up from his preferred lounging position. "Stalin was responsible for the death of at least twenty million people. That's a conservative estimation. And yet the name Joseph has never dropped in popularity."

"And why is that?" asked Alice.

"Because Joseph is a much more ubiquitous and internationally known name, much more integral to the popular vernacular. Often a family name. It is too complicated to extricate a name like that from public use. So, people play at moral consciousness, but selectively. It's the popularity bias. They want to seem politically and socially aware but not at any meaningful cost to their personal conveniences," said Corinne.

She did that often. Quietly waited on the sidelines of the conversation, interjecting only when she felt her contribution was too meaningful not to.

"I think there's too much attachment to words in modern culture," said Zilla, ever the provocateur. "Granted it isn't as draconian as at the peak of the political correctness zeitgeist of the '20s and '30s, but it's still pretty restrictive."

I clapped my hands together. "Yeah, I know, we're definitely going with an unknown."

"With the world ending, you'd think the geniuses who might potentially save it would have other things to talk about than phrasing things just right in the most inoffensive manner possible," said Brent, twisting his lips into a displeased expression.

Brent has changed his focus three times already. His latest was politics, but he was contemplating comparative theology. There was hunger in him, but also a certain anger. Something he always held tightly in check, but over the years, you learned to recognize it. Brent's father thought he was the Antichrist and tried to kill him. It was a famous case. All things considered, Brent came out relatively normal. For all his intelligence, Brent was sometimes difficult to talk to, too combative. The guy, it seemed, was always gearing up for a fight.

"Is it geniuses or genii?" Ton asked, always the guy to throw some water on the fire at just the right time.

"Technically both," Corinne responded. "Genius is actually from the Latin word meaning a protective spirit or an innate ability. So Latin pluralization applies. Genii is so seldom used it makes people think of genie as in Djinn. Which, though also a sort of spirit, is Arabic and thus a different thing altogether."

I loved it when she talked about words. I only ever learned the three languages mandated by the curriculum. But I loved to read, I loved words, and she knew more about them than anyone I've ever met.

"So, what would you name a planet?" I asked her.

"Why, Corinne, of course." She winked at me.

It was one of those times when I desperately wished I had scored higher on my EIQ (emotional intelligence quotient) assessment.

No way of knowing if she's serious, outside of directly asking her. What if she does mean it? Is that something worth doing? I've thought of a name for my mystery planet for so long, but never came up with anything definitive. I've dreamt of a name like Arrokoth, which to me had long been synonymous with the farthest reaches of space. Of imagination itself.

And what if I took Corinne along with me? Would it mean the same as naming a planet after her?

I should ask Zilla. Zilla scored much higher than me on EIQ, though he has never shown much interest in conventional romantic pursuits.

Maybe I should ask my dad.

I seldom thought about my dad as a serious discussion partner. It sounds conceited to say now, it may come across as distant and even mean, but it was never like that. He simply ... wasn't on my level. We could do small talk easily enough, but when it came to grand ideas, those I saved for my friends. Was I being unfair to him the entire time? Should I have made more of an effort to include him in my life?

I don't have enough real-life examples of this, but books and media have led me to believe that parent/child relationships are profoundly complex and often hinge upon strategically withholding information. It seems like a thing mostly done to spare one's feelings as opposed to the three-digit numerical difference in IQs, but it's definitely a thing.

Now that we are apart much further physically than we ever were mentally or emotionally, I find I think about my dad more. I try to imagine what life must have been like for him. How different it was compared to me. Both as a young man and as an adult.

I am here with my friends, the smartest people in the known world, on the most advanced spacecraft ever built on the way to a distant planet I discovered, a planet that may be the future of humanity. And he is back home, alone, with nothing but menial labor and old TV shows and an occasional whiskey to show for his days. That can't be the life he wanted. The life he dreamed of.

Alas, this is getting unwelcomingly maudlin. I am ending this blog. Genie, please create a reminder for me to write to my dad in the next day or two.

"Reminder set, Dar".

DARYL

One time I made the mistake of telling my kid his mom would have been proud of him. I never forgot the look on his face.

"Dad," he said quietly as if struggling to control emotion, "she doesn't matter."

It was harsh. Winter harsh was the expression I once read in a novel, one of those perfect descriptions. Brutal to hear. But I had learned to understand him by then. And I knew that outside of cheap sentimentality, there was indeed no value in bringing his mother up to him. She was never important to him in any way that mattered. A failed mother, a failed wife, and then a failed person. Tragically weak, I suppose is how he saw her.

But I worried about him then, worried if he would go through life assessing everyone with a dispassionate eye, assigning people value and worth based on his own preconceived and most likely impossibly high value metrics. I didn't want him to be alone, I didn't want him to be lonely. I wanted him to have more than his studies.

I think I stopped worrying about that the day I met Corinne. I've seen the girl around the Lyceum, but Daryl never talked about her any more than he did about his other schoolmates, and, in retrospect, I appreciated my son's discretion. It seemed like a sign of maturity, the foretelling of the man he'd grow into. And then one day, he asked if he could bring her over for Thanksgiving. Corinne, being Belgian, he explained, didn't celebrate and was curious about the tradition.

I cleaned the house top to bottom and did my best to prepare a vegan feast to dazzle the young lady. If she wasn't dazzled, she hid it well. She was a lovely girl, and the evening went very well in my estimation, but what I remember the most from it is my son's face when he looked at Corinne. He was in love with her, that much was obvious. I didn't know if he knew it yet, though I found it difficult to believe my son wouldn't be aware of something that seemed so plain to me, so beautifully obvious.

For me, it was a much welcome confirmation that there was a heart behind all that brain, that my kid wouldn't go through years alone, that there'd be more to his life.

I don't think I've ever looked at anyone the way he looked at Corinne. I don't think I've ever felt about anyone that way, which explains a lot about my life.

Here I am, alone, peering through a telescope in my backyard. Trying to imagine where my son might be right now.

"Dad," I can almost hear him chastising me, "You can't possibly expect to see me with this aperture."

I know, kiddo, I know, but I can dream.

My own parents weren't especially parental. Or they were, once upon a time, with my older sister, but by the time I came along, unplanned, and much too late, they were pretty spent on the parental front. They did all the work, checked all the boxes, but tiredly, unenthusiastically, at best dutifully going through the motions.

I was never close with my sister, too much of an age difference. I'm not close with her now. Last I heard, she was somewhere in Utah. She sold cosmetics for a while, married an accountant, never had any kids. Neither she nor my parents ever took to Daryl, the kindest way to put it is that he gave them the creeps. Too unconventional for such conventional mindsets. No, we were not a close family by any means.

My sister and I haven't seen each other since burying our parents. They died a while back, gradually shrinking themselves out of this life, it seems, getting smaller and smaller until one day they got too weak to go on and took advantage of the euthanasia release.

Release is a strange word for it, but that's how it's marketed. As if this life is a kind of prison, with green grass and blue skies just outside. I don't think I'd want that for myself, but who knows what the future holds. I'd hate to be useless, helpless, a deadweight to society, to Daryl.

Every so often a terrifying thought occurs to me, one I do my best to chase it away: What if I outlive my son? What if he doesn't return?

This mission he's on, he has assured me of its safety, so has his friend Zilla, so has Corinne. These kids, they have it all planned out. They aren't even kids anymore, of course. They are young people, remarkable young people. If anyone can build a spaceship, travel to a distant planet, and get back safely, it's them. But what if, just *what if* it's actually impossible? What if the people who have, always, thought of every possible thing, didn't think of something? What if that something goes wrong? Too wrong? What if this ultimate test of their intelligence, their will, their power turns out to be too difficult? Or rigged somehow?

I don't think I could bear it.

Never thought I'd be one of those parents who live for their kids and define themselves through their kids, but it's true what they say: this is the only immortality we can be granted in this life. For me, it is.

For Daryl... well, Daryl and his friends get to create their own immortality.

DAR

I chose to stay awake for most of this trip. I didn't have to, but I couldn't imagine entering any of the phases of sleep for the duration. I didn't want to miss a thing. I'm a proverbial kid on the night before Christmas, too excited to sleep.

Others opted for different rest phases. Corinne wakes every five days, Zilla every seven. The rest alternates. It's a sound decision that optimizes economy. I am alone, but never lonely.

For the longest time, I didn't understand the difference between the two. Definitionally, sure, but not in any practical way. The first time it occurred to me was while watching an old crime drama with Zilla. What was it? Aha, *The Heat.* In it, one of the characters discusses the difference while talking to a potential, much younger love interest.

'It's the Hollywood Fifteen," Zilla told me.

"What is?"

"The age difference. Customary for mainstream movies. Sometimes twenty. The male is always older."

"Why? Doesn't it limit the life experiences and cultural references they can possibly share?" It seemed so strange to me; everyone I knew was around my age. Corinne was exactly my age.

"I'm not sure. It may have been a display of patriarchy."

We were seldom alone or lonely at the Lyceum. The Habs were shared. There were always people at the Bibliotheca, which most still referred to as simply the library or Bib. There were always people in the otium. There was plenty to do, plenty to learn, plenty to discuss.

You have to imagine how large the Lyceum was. Not just a school, it was a small town onto itself with all the concomitant conveniences. And, to many of us back then, our entire world. At its height, there were so many kids attending, you could very well meet someone new on a frequent basis. I wasn't the most socially adventurous person, then or now, so I stuck with my steady group of friends, with Corinne. But there were a lot of us, geniuses, roaming the Lyceum.

Every so often, someone would make the news for either a scientific breakthrough or some kind of an invention or a new record set, and they'd become briefly famous, but it took a lot to stand out among the Chosen, and the popularity typically only lasted until the next great thing came along.

Seldom did anyone gain fame for something other than that, but when they did, it was noticed. Which is why when Mal got expelled, it was all anyone could talk about.

Mal, Malcolm Armstrong IV, was a scion of a family so stratospherically wealthy that their worth was a subject of jealous awe and wild speculation. They could have paid for the entire Lyceum in fact, not merely the Bib wing, with just the change from their couch cushions. That's a funny expression Zilla taught me, and it is the first time I'm using it. What do you think, Genie?

"Very nice, Dar. Albeit somewhat dated due to the use of the anachronistic coinage reference."

Okay, then. Moving on.

Because of the Armstrongs' wealth, Mal got away with a lot. Until eventually he managed to do something so terrible that even his family could not buy his way out of it. No one was sure what that something was. There were rumors and speculations, but nothing you'd want to give credence to without facts.

There were rumors about what became of Mal since, too, but again, only rumors.

The loudest ones postulated he joined the Shunned.

"What do you think happened?"

"I heard he raped someone," said Alice.

"Date raped?" asked Brent.

"What's the difference?" Alice sneered at him. "Rape is rape."

"There was an ugly culture of date rape on normi campuses for ages," said Zilla. "Probably still is."

"Should have judged the book by the proverbial cover. That name, Mal. It means evil, from Latin, but also used in French and Spanish to signify something terrible, something wrong," said Corinne.

"He was one of my best customers," offered Ton from his favorite chair, the memory foam of which has long been molded to his seemingly boneless form. "But I don't miss the guy. Always was a creep."

"Does anyone know what he was working on?" I asked.

"Actually, a lot of the similar things you guys are. Quantum physics and intergalactic travel." Brent nodded his perfectly coifed head in my and Zilla's direction. Of all of us he knew Mal the best. Their families went ways back, though Brent's family was nowhere near the Armstrongs in wealth or power.

"That's a shame. All that knowledge ..."

"I heard he went to live with the Shunned. Underground," said Ollie. Ollie came to our group later but integrated himself so seamlessly that soon it was difficult to imagine he wasn't always there. An almost annoyingly cheerful Canadian with a mop of blonde hair and a sunny smile, he looked like a surfer or a TV star, but was in fact the foremost expert in zoology, minoring in xenobiology and sidelining in cryptozoology. Just to have all the bases covered, as he jokingly explained it.

We seldom talked about the Shunned. It wasn't a done thing.

"Shh." Zilla winked. "Remember the first rule about the Shunned?   We don't talk about the Shunned."

Of course, we remembered. Zilla has made us watch *Fight Club* more than once. It was a cult classic, according to him. Corinne defined it, less flatteringly, as a testosterone-fueled vile fantasy of the toxicity of male aggression. "They cannot contain the violence they view as their biological imperative, so they resort to this," she explained, her lip curling in disgust, adorable in her self-righteousness. I wasn't much of a media critic and thought the movie was somewhere in between the vile fantasy and a classic. Then again, Zilla always says all media is essentially social commentary if viewed smartly.

I apologize for the digression, let's get back on track. The Shunned.

We did talk about the Shunned. How could you not? They were the obverse side of the coin. The us that might have been. The parallel universe made reality.

Why don't I talk about it now? For posterity if nothing else. In the interest of presenting a well-rounded blog account of my life and my times. Because, while the Shunned were never a part of my life, what we shared was thicker than blood. We shared a mutation.

Amartium was banned almost immediately after the side effects were discovered. I am referring to the stillborn rates, the death statistics. Our mutations were discovered much later and correlated later still. And yet, the product remained circulating in the dark waters of the underground economy for years to come, some say decades. It existed as a nonentity until the Chosen became a known factor, and then its popularity skyrocketed. People, it seems, were willing to risk their lives and the lives of their unborn babies, all to give them something they could never have offered them otherwise: a chance at greatness.

It's difficult to say if the Amartium available then was pure or altered. I'd imagine altered, but there simply isn't enough data available. A lot of these people, their births were off the record, underground, secret. It is said the death rates were higher. It is said the mutation rates were more varied, and they didn't just include the brains. But eventually, a new generation of baby geniuses was out there in the world, and since their very existence was a byproduct of illegality, they didn't rate as high on anyone's priority lists. Not like us, never like us. They weren't invited or accepted to the Lyceum. Their upbringing, so often outside the law, made the public think of them as dangerous, unpredictable, volatile.

There was a public outcry to count these individuals, track them, possibly tame them, possibly use them. They wanted none of it, these new kids. Of course, they didn't. And so, they went underground. Supporting themselves by any means necessary, they took to hacking and things of that nature.

There was a dedicated team of the Chosen at the Lyceum just to deal with the ever-increasing number of cyber threats and create stronger firewalls and protections.

Everyone agrees these individuals are dangerous, but their off-the-grid existence and guerilla tactics make them difficult to find and prosecute. They exist as an ever-present threat, but in a world as imperiled as ours, a world where nuclear agreements are casually dissolved, and people are killed over essential resources, on a planet that seems determined to wipe the civilization off its face, the Shunned are only one threat out of many. They've learned to stay out of sight and thus largely out of mind. But they are always somewhere, plotting, planning.

Their illegally bought IQs; their ostracized lives some say made for dark souls. They are the ultimate outcasts. Distrusted, feared, shunned. The latter was turned into their moniker and stuck. The Shunned.

If Mal had joined them, he'd be in good company. Good as in apt, since there'd be nothing good about the situation. People become their company, according to most social studies out there. They can choose the right people and be elevated by them or choose wrongly and be dragged down into the abyss.

It was all too dark to contemplate.

"Changing the subject," announced Zilla.

"To?"

"Oh, I don't know," he prevaricated, by now well and truly mellowed out on Ton's latest strand. "How about the treatment of the grandfather paradox in the old-time travel movies?"

Ollie laughed "Watch out, people. He's going to make us watch *The Terminator* again."

"You should be so lucky. Those movies are classics."

"Those movies are silly," said Alice. "But they follow their own internal logic, however flawed, with admirable consistency."

"Until that last one." Ton piped up. "That one made no sense."

"It did if you followed the plot and didn't take a nap halfway through," countered Zilla.

"The movie that played in my mind during my nap made more sense." Ton smirked. "I have very logical dreams."

I should ask him if he still does. My dreams have been all over the place here on the ship. They disappear upon waking up before I can analyze them properly, but both my EEG and EKG show fascinating levels of sleepcycle activity. Something to discuss with our onboard psychologist, perhaps. In fact, Genie, set an appointment for me to chat with Yumi during her next awake cycle".

"Will do, Dar."

DARYL

The Lyceum isn't what it used to be. The kids have grown up. It is now less of a school and more of a research center. They still need my services and I'm happy enough to provide them, but the change was tough for me. At first, I thought I was merely missing my son, but then I realized I was also missing the continuing education, the ceaseless intellectual pushing and shoving of the ideas in my brain, fueled by the classes I frequented. So, I did the only logical thing—Aristotle and Daryl Jr. would be proud—and enrolled in night school.

Now I'm taking classes of my own. No longer standing in the back of auditoriums, I'm sitting near the front of the classrooms. I'm learning things. I'm back to having homework assignments, a strange and welcome regression that gives my nights and weekends some much-needed structure.

Space travel when powered by the combined genius of the smartest people on Earth is considerably shorter in duration than it would have been otherwise. In fact, Daryl's friend Zilla once told me it would have taken three generations to get to their destination if not for that antimatter/matter thingie he cooked up. Yes, I know, *thingie*. I shouldn't say that. One of the many reasons to stick to higher learning.

As is, their journey will take years. A fraction of the original estimate, but still a long time. The way I figure, by the time Daryl comes back, and I don't dare to entertain any other possibility, I shall have at least one college degree with my name, our name, on it to show him. My kid has made me proud his entire life, it's time I did something to return the favor.

I imagine the look on his face. Like many of the Chosen, he isn't given to overt emotion, but over the years I learned to read and appreciate his subtle expressions. Pride will be a new one for me, and I'm looking forward to it.

The classes I'm taking aren't nearly as difficult as I was afraid they would be. I'm guessing it's due to all the ones I've semi-clandestinely frequented at the Lyceum. And yes, of course, I am majoring in astronomy. *Ad Astra* as Daryl would say, which is Latin for *To the Stars*. It is the only destination.

I never would have met Sonya if not for night school. And my faulty memory. Here's how it happened.

It was a rainy fall evening, and I jogged to my car —my jacket over my head, my bookbag awkwardly bouncing against my back—only to realize upon arrival that its battery was hopelessly and irrevocably dead.

That's the thing with technology, isn't it? You can invent the best tech there is, but it'll still be prone to human error. Which is to say there was nothing wrong with my car's solar outside of the idiot who completely forgot to charge it.

I stood there, letting frustration take over, considering the alternatives, and then felt a tap on my shoulder. It was a woman wearing a red anorak, a woman whose face I recognized from school, but didn't have a name readily available in my mind to put to it. I was sure we shared at least one class, which only added to my embarrassment.

"Happens to me at least once every couple of months." She smiled, gesturing at the dead car situation. "And I even set reminders for myself."

"Old age is no joke." I smiled back, ruefully shaking my head.

"Come on," she said, "I'll give you a ride. You can come back for your car later with a charged backup."

I readily agreed. Random acts of kindness are a rare thing and should be appreciated when offered.

"I'm just over there," she nodded at the next lane over.

We walked to her car. I gave up on the undignified rain jog, glad to soon be out of the weather.

"I'm Sonya," she said.

"Hi, Sonya, I'm Daryl."

"I know. We have physics together."

Ah, *physics.*

"Sorry," I said, genuinely. "My memory's crap."

"As evidenced by the dead car solar." She nodded, unfazed.

"As evidenced by the dead car solar."

Sonya drove something larger than a car, more of a van. There was a logo on the side, but the rain streaks and the late hour had made it all but illegible. We got in, and she switched the heat on right away, then rummaged in the back and produced a towel for me.

"Thank you."

"You're welcome. So where to?"

I gave her my address.

"You live on the actual Lyceum grounds?"

"Yes, I am the caretaker there." I may be rusty, but I wasn't about to call myself a janitor in front of a pretty lady. And she was pretty, though not in an easily obvious kind of way like Annie was, wild hair and a glint of danger in her eyes, and not in a flawless way like Corinne is, who looks like she just walked out of a frame, art come to life. Sonya had a lived-in kind of prettiness, one shaped and formed by her years and experiences. Maybe I'm not explaining it right. I'm no

Shakespeare, though I am taking a class on him next semester. What he has to do with astronomy I may never know, but it's something to do with a well-rounded education.

I guess what I'm trying to say is that Sonya looked like someone pleased and comfortable in their own skin, in their own life. It made for a certain glow to her features, a certain draw to her smile. And her eyes, they were the kindest eyes I ever saw.

It's funny the things you notice about women at different stages of your life. The things that attract you. I don't think kindness was very high on the list of attributes I looked for in a woman when I was a young man, which explains a lot. But now, it was ... it was perfect.

Sonya's eyes didn't stay the same color, either, though I didn't learn that until later. They changed, depending on her mood, on ambient light, on the clothes and jewelry she wore, from green to grey to, occasionally, a light shade of blue. It was kind of like magic, I told her, her own personal brand of magic.

But that all came later.

That night as she saved my sorry, soaked and saggy self from the rain like some knight errant, she was still a stranger to me, nothing but a kind stranger.

"Do you know the way?" I asked her.

"Yes." She sighed. "I know the way."

Why the sigh? I wondered but didn't ask.

We made small talk, mostly about our studies. She was friendly, nice, charming even with a slight undercurrent of sadness beneath it all I couldn't quite place and wouldn't until later.

When she dropped me off, she handed me a small cardboard box from the back.

"Something to brighten up your evening."

"Oh, you've already done too much," I protested.

"Just take it." She shoved it at me unceremoniously. "You'll be happy you did."

I thanked her again, took my gift, and got out of her van.

"See you in class, Sonya."

"See you in class, Daryl."

When I got home, I put the box on the table and immediately got out of my wet clothes and took a shower. I never liked the rain unless I'm home for the night with nowhere to go and it's raging outside, providing a perfect ambiance for a horror movie or something.

Freshly showered, towel-dried, and comfortable in my favorite pair of sweats and an old tee, I remembered the box and opened it. Inside there was a muffin. A perfectly baked, perfectly shaped muffin, a huge one, almost a small cake onto itself. It smelled divine.

I didn't realize how hungry I was. I devoured the entire thing standing over the table, forgetting to sit down. I'm not one for describing tastes, but it was easily the best muffin I ever had. The best baked good I ever had.

My mother didn't bake, favoring the premade store-bought goods. Corinne did bake occasionally and brought me things, but her flavor combinations were always too wild, too exotic for my plain old tastebuds. This muffin was perfection.

I figured out what the logo on the side of Sonya's van was. She had to have been a baker.

I waited patiently for our next physics class together and, after it was over, marshaling all my courage, came up to Sonya and asked her out.

"Guess you really liked the muffin?" she joked.

"Maybe I just really like the baker." I shrugged in mock nonchalance. "Go out with me and find out."

This wasn't like me at all. She must have brought it out in me, this strange newfound confidence. I was hoping it would stick around but turned out I didn't need it much. Being with Sonya was easy in all the right ways. She was kind, funny, smart. The warmth of her personality smoothed over any of that getting-to-know-you awkwardness of new relationships.

"We're too old for all that drama," she'd tell me. She was, in fact, five years older than me. We were at an age when it couldn't have possibly mattered, but she liked to joke about it all the same.

"I'm a cougar," Sonya would joke. Which is apparently a really dated term for older women dating younger men. She had a penchant for old TV shows and vintage mystery novels. She said she liked them before all the graphic violence became the norm in popular media, yet she agreed to watch the show I was named after, provided I read some Agatha Christie.

Wouldn't you know it, we both got the better end of the deal out of that arrangement. Don't think I've ever read so many books by the same author and enjoyed them that much, but Christie, that lady knew what she was doing.

And, of course, there were baked goods. Many, many baked goods. I put on weight, and Sonya said it looked good on me, that I was too gaunt before.

"Like dating Ichabod Crane," she'd say, leaving me to figure out the reference.

"You'd think we met in a literature class," I'd grumble but play along.

The main thing is I was happy. I *am* happy. All the more so for finding such an unexpected and unplanned sort of happiness. It takes me out of my head, distracts me from missing Daryl, gives me something more to live for and look forward to other than my son's return. In a way, I suppose, it's finally given me a life of my own.

DAR

The year I was born an Italian astronomer named Mario Alessandro Bellini discovered a new galaxy.

He named it Venezia del Mare, after his hometown that sank beneath the waves, the sea that consumed it, and as a play on words after his own name, since his childhood nickname was Mare.

I remember seeing it for the first time and feeling a strange tug in my heart, like a gravitational shift. It was as if somehow I knew that among those newly discovered celestial bodies one would prove to be my ultimate destination.

I digitized the ceiling projections in our Hab to only show me Venezia del Mare. I spent countless hours staring up at it, dreaming of solving its secrets. Until one day I did.

But this memory, this is from a time before that. Me and Zilla were getting high. I believe Ton was there too, never the one to miss out on the opportunity to sample his own product with friends and hear its praises sung.

I was lying on the floor, staring up at the ceiling, the carpet synthfibers hugging me like tall grass.

Zilla reconfigured his bed into a recliner and was busy telling us of yet another failed romance. Or, I suppose I should say affair or dalliance, since due to Zilla's fairly emotionless and pragmatic demeanor, his involvements were always less of a romantic and more of a carnal nature.

"What'd you expect, man?" Ton shrugged. "She was a normi."

Yes, some of us occasionally dated the normis. It was unavoidable, in a way, since for some inexplicable reason Amartium produced much higher rates of baby boys than baby girls. The ratios were off and, if one was to pursue a heterosexual romance, the normis seems like a viable way to go.

It never worked out, though. Not in the long run.

Once the initial thrill and rush of chemicals wore off, you were often left with someone you really couldn't talk to. Plus, there were all the social ramifications to consider.

It wasn't taboo, by any means. There was no actual stigma attached as such, but the matter was contemptuous at best.

Normis isn't exactly an affectionate term. Genies, they'd sneer back at us. Much has been said about the inherent inferiority/superiority dichotomy of our arrangement. There were numerous studies. In fact, our very own onboard psychologist extraordinaire, Yumi, has written a definitive paper on it and is considered the topmost expert on the subject.

Other people, they hated us, I think. And yet needed us. And hated us for needing us. They needed us to save them from themselves. From their ruined planet. From their meaningless and angry lives. And yet they hated being helpless, hated depending on us.

They hungrily took advantage of every invention we produced to ease and improve their existence, while casually disregarding all the warnings we made about the future, the same way they did with climate change many decades earlier.

They were intrigued by us and they were repelled by us. We looked just like them and we were nothing like them.

We were their champions, but they anticipated our missteps eagerly to pounce on us. We were their saviors and yet they longed to crucify us for not saving them fast enough.

A lot of this came to a head during the last few years. The discovery of the planet we're headed to wasn't merely a necessity, it was a perfect PR move. Give the public the shiny ship, tell them it'll eventually take them away from all the mess they've made, offer them hope.

We heard it all, we knew it all, we worked under crippling amounts of pressure, and we succeeded. Now here we are.

And for all the generalizations I've made about the normis, I wasn't wrong. Then again, it was never meant to be a perfect world. We came too late into it. But maybe, just maybe, the perfect world is what awaits us, the proverbial tabula rasa. I can't wait to find out.

That was an exceptionally discursive digression. I didn't know I had it in me. Perhaps talking to Yumi the other day brought it up.

She says my dreams are spurred on by my reminiscences. I'm triggering specific areas of the brain, making them work harder, while others, the normally overworked ones, are getting more downtime. I'm not going to go into specifics, but it does make sense. And Yumi would know—no one knows more about brains than Yumi.

She and her brother, Yoshi, were the only Japanese kids at the Lyceum. Japan was generally skeptical of all Western poisons during the time of their birth, so Amartium never made it there, but Yumi and Yoshi's father was an international diplomat living in the US at the time, and their mother just happened to have excessive nausea during her pregnancy. Et voila. Two of them, the rare Chosen Twins as they were known.

Yoshi grew up to be obsessed with computers. He may well be singlehandedly responsible for securing the most critical global servers from the attacks by the Shunned. It's an all-encompassing obsession for him. For a while, he wouldn't even go outside. Yumi said he was being a hikikomori, a uniquely Japanese sort of a recluse. The thing is, Yoshi's ultimate goal was to disappear into a computer, shed the bounds of this mortal coil, and become pure disembodied consciousness. For all I know he might have succeeded with his goal had we not dragged him with us on this mission. It was Yumi's idea, she knew he wouldn't be able to resist the challenge. Merely designing our computer systems, including the inimitable Genie, top to bottom, wouldn't be enough for Yoshi.

And so, he's here on the ship, awake, like me, typing away, I hear him in his cabin, but dare not disturb him. Who knows what magic he's up to in there? Yoshi, traditionally, sees no one but Yumi. Yumi sees everyone and dispenses advice with the practiced ease and steady calm of someone who has unraveled every mystery of every curvature of the human brain. Yumi has a strikingly inscrutable face, and her hair always stays preternaturally perfect. Corinne, prone to helmet head—which I find charming, and she categorically doesn't—says she'd kill for Yumi's hair. If a humorless person is listening to or reading this blog in the future, she doesn't mean it literally.

And so, digressive as I am today, I return to my original memory of getting high with my friends.

Zilla, for all his occasional dating impetuousness, was easily consolable. In fact, he already began moving on to discussing old *X-Men* comics. A transition that might have seemed random to anyone who didn't know him, but was, in fact, quintessential Zilla.

"The mutant to non-mutant dynamics in those comic books and movies are a perfect correlation to the Chosen/normis situation. People have always hated anyone different, especially anyone potentially superior to them. That's why the first movie's opening scene at the concentration camp is so effective. It underscores that entire theme of the impossible balance. The ultimate in love/hate relationships."

If left alone, Zilla could go on about this for hours and eventually make us watch the movies to highlight his points. And we've seen all those movies, more than once. I agreed with Zilla, the parallels were obvious, but I didn't care for media repetitions.

"I think someone's been in our Hab," I said, changing the subject. "Someone who wasn't supposed to."

"Oh no, poor bear." Ton laughed. "Is my product giving you the Goldilocks?"

To give someone the Goldilocks in Ton's speak is to make someone paranoid. Yes, he had to explain it to us. No one got the reference originally. Ton had some obscure ones under his belt, his cultural anthropology research feeding his passion for them.

"I'm serious, though," I insisted. "I really think someone might have snuck a peek at my research."

"So get Yoshi to up your encryptions," said Zilla, dismissively. "I'm sure it's nothing, though. Who'd risk that?"

Who would indeed? The Lyceum had a very strict code of honor when it came to personal and intellectual property. The code was enforced, and its breaches were punishable. Ruffling through someone's nowhere-near-finished research certainly didn't seem worth it. Maybe I *was* just being paranoid. After all, I seldom partook in Ton's offerings.

I sighed. "This is why I shouldn't get high."

"Nah, I just gotta get you on a different strand." Ton stretched his loose-limbed body, got up, and reached for his screen. "Now let's sort out some snacks."

Why am I thinking about that now? That memory has mostly made me realize how hungry I am. I should go eat something and get ready. Corinne will be waking up soon from her sleepcycle for our weekend together. If it is, indeed, the weekend. It's difficult to maintain an accurate record of time here.

"Genie, will you kindly print me some food."

"What would you like, Dar?"

"Oh, nothing too elaborate, maybe some sandwich cubes and a nutrimilk."

"Any dessert, Dar?"

"I don't know, Genie. Have you learned to print a perfect muffin yet?"

There was a bakery in town, not too far from the Lyceum, that made perfect muffins. One of those things Zilla affectionately, if only slightly condescendingly, referred to as the normi magic. I've been trying to get Genie to create a perfect reproduction. It hasn't happened yet, but I'm not giving up.

"You know I don't respond to sarcasm, Dar."

"I'm sorry, Genie. Yes, let's do a muffin for dessert."

"I've been working on bran and very berry."

"I'll try both," I say. I am, after all, nothing if not adventurous.

DARYL

The first time Sonya finds out about my last name she does a double-take I was getting used to by now.

"Like Daryl Olsen, the space guy?"

"The one and only."

"Aren't you too old to be named for him?" She squints at me, jokingly.

"I'm so old that he's named for me, actually."

"What? No. Is he really your kid? Jokes aside, you don't seem old enough to have a kid that age."

I shrug. "Had him young."

"You must be very proud."

"I am," I agree. "Every day. Best son a man can ask for."

"Not to mention the potential savior of humankind." She winks.

"There's that, but as he always tells me, it's a team effort."

"He made the discovery."

"Yes, but without his best friend they'd have no means of getting there anytime soon."

"Here." I walk over to my overflowing bookshelf. It's an old-fashioned indulgence to hold on to paper books, but I do it anyway. These days so few even get printed. If they do, they are usually special commemorative editions of the most significant works. My son's book is there. I place my fingers gently on its midnight-sky-blue cover, trace the debossed letters of his name, our name. I never get tired of it.

I hand Sonya the book.

"*Post Tenebra Lux* by Daryl Olsen," she reads out loud. "I heard about it. Now I have no excuse not to read it."

I grin at her. "None whatsoever."

She reads it. She likes it. She asks me many questions about it. Questions I'm proud to say my ever-increasing knowledge of astronomy is letting me answer more and more eloquently and elaborately.

"What about you?" I ask, referring to her choice of major. "Why history?"

"Well." She sighs. "You see all this?" She points to the media screen playing on the opposite wall. It's set to the news. I don't know why—it's relentlessly depressing, but I feel a strong compulsion to follow.

We watch the highlights for a minute in silence. There are more deadly drone strikes in the latest Middle East conflict. Another small island chain in the

Pacific has surrendered to the rising ocean. An earthquake in Japan has devastated Okinawa. There was a mysterious explosion at a former space rocket launch site in Nunavut. The death toll is rising in the drought wars in Western Africa.

I force myself to look away.

"Well, that's why," Sonya says, quietly. "Because of all these things. I want to learn, want to understand how we got to this, collectively as a civilization."

I nod. "I get it."

"I know it doesn't matter, I know it might be too late," she says. "I just want to make sense of it for myself, in my mind."

"One of Daryl's friends used to have this theory that it was inevitable. That we are self-destructive as species."

"Genetically?"

"More like..." I think of what Brent used to say. "More like we were an experiment with an expiration date. But the Earth was always meant to reclaim itself back from us. It was only a matter of time."

"That's rather morbid."

"I know. This wasn't a close friend of Daryl's. They only hung out for a short while. I don't know what became of that kid and his theories."

"Isn't it strange we still call them kids?" Sonya says. "They are all adults now."

"Yeah, isn't it something? The way our kids remain our kids forever, and all of this Chosen and Shunned business just falls away?"

Sonya's quiet for a while. Serious. Looks like she's gearing up to say something heavy.

I wait. I like that I've come to know her looks. There's great comfort in knowing someone that well, in letting yourself be known like that by someone. We haven't been together for that long, but it seems like it's been years. In a good way. In a comfortable lived-in way.

I know there are still things we don't know about each other, but I have faith that all will be revealed in its own good time.

"My youngest was one of the Chosen," Sonya finally says, so quietly I have to strain to hear it. She's never talked about her kids before. I knew she had two. I gathered they weren't around, probably permanently so, but never figured out a way to ask.

"A boy or a girl?"

"A girl. Usually, the first pregnancy is the tough one, but with me, it was the second. Absolutely brutal. My husband heard about Amartium. And eight months later, we were the proud parents of a bouncing baby girl with no idea that she's going to outsmart us all someday." She pauses. "Didn't do the tests until late. Thought she was just, you know, precocious. Then she started doing her older sister's homework, high school homework, and we knew it was more than that."

"She tested off the charts, especially in math. The Lyceum invited her to come study. We couldn't say no. They gave us enough financial assistance to relocate closer to the school so that we could see her more often. It was fine, for a while. Even good, maybe. Megan, that was her name, Megan was thriving. We didn't even notice how hard it hit our other daughter, Cassie."

She pauses again. Takes a breath and holds it, then lets it out slowly, yoga style. All I can do is wait. I don't think this story is headed anyplace happy.

"Cassie couldn't understand, couldn't accept how much smarter her baby sister was. How much attention her baby sister got. Cassie was a good kid, popular, fun, but never really academically exceptional. She did terribly on her SATs, failed to get into a university. Had to stay here, do community college, and work with me at the bakery. While Megan was in the news for setting another record, solving another unsolvable math puzzle, proving another unprovable theorem. Maybe it was our fault, maybe we gave Megan too much attention, maybe the balance was off, but we loved them both. Always. I'd tell that to the girls all the time, but at some point, I think Cassie stopped believing me."

Another pause. Another sigh tinged with regret. The tears stay unshed, brimming in the corners of her eyes.

"Cassie got into drinking. Then worse things. She started stealing from the bakery's register, staying out late, partying with all the wrong sorts. We were worried but didn't know how to address it. My husband was more of an Old Testament or at least old-world kind of man. A first-generation immigrant from the old country, he wanted to lay down the law heavy-handedly. I stopped him. Said she'll be alright; she'll find her way. How stupid I was." Sonya shakes her head.

"Anyway, one day over the Christmas holidays, Megan is with us. Cassie's home. There's Christmas music, we got a tree. We are a normal family for once. I'm preparing the food. Ivan, that was my husband's name, is napping in his favorite recliner. The girls are watching something on the living room screen last I checked. I'm about to ask them to help me with the cookies, and then I notice they're not there. Moreover, it's way too quiet. "Girls," I call. Search the house. Find them in the bathroom. There's blood, so much blood ..."

Sonya cuts off. The tears that were brimming her lashes spill over. She's crying now, heavily but silently, her shoulders are shaking. I put my arms around her. I can't imagine that sort of grief. What she's been living with.

When she resumes her story, she does something like a brief summary. Just trying to get it all out. Turns out Cassie went to the bathroom to get high, and when Megan tried to stop her, Cassie pushed her away. Probably didn't mean to push so hard but did it all the same. Exactly the wrong way, too. Just one of those things. The poor kid hit her head on a washing machine corner at the worst possible angle. Cassie OD'd looking at the dead body of her baby sister. A terrible tragedy that played out impossibly quickly and quietly. Something that shouldn't happen, ever. And yet...

Ivan left not long after that. Some couples are brought together by grief, some are torn apart by it. If he blamed Sonya for being too soft with Cassie, he didn't say. He was never a man of many words. He left a life he felt was ruined and promptly drank himself into an early grave. Death by grief and vodka.

Sonya stayed. I think about it. Somehow, she found the strength to carry on. To continue baking, smiling, living. I don't know if I would have in her place. What a woman, I think. I hold her, kiss her hair, whisper *I'm sorrys* into it.

And in the back of my mind, I'm thinking about Daryl. Thinking about how fortunate I am that he turned out the way he did. Hoping he's happy right now. He must be getting closer. What it must be like to actually get to live out your dreams.

DAR

The first person I told was Corinne. We were lying in my bed, alone in the Hab. Zilla was away visiting his family. I have a very clear mental picture of that morning, it's one of my favorite memories. The sun was making its way through the window, and the space smelled of freshly laundered sheets, Corinne's citrusy shampoo, and the vague stale mustiness of sleep. I've been awake for a while, just watching Corinne's face. She always looked perfectly serene when sleeping even if later she told me she had been having nightmares. Finally, she stirred, opened one eye, and looked at me.

"Are you watching me sleep?"

I nodded, smiling.

"You're such a creep," she said and tried to whack me with her pillow. Her hand-to-eye coordination was nowhere near awake enough to pull off that move, so she sighed and rolled over, away from me. "I must look a mess."

"You look beautiful."

She rubbed the sleep out of her eyes and sat up.

"You're such a flatterer." She kissed my chin. "How long have you been up?"

"A while."

"Couldn't sleep?"

I shook my head. "I found it," I said quietly.

"You … found it delightful how well we fit together?" she joked, trying to gather her hair into a semblance of a ponytail.

"No." I laughed. "But also, yes, of course."

"You found my audibuds, so I don't have to listen to you snore all night?"

"I have no idea where you put your audibuds, and I categorically do not snore."

"Well then?" She looked at me expectantly, her freshly assembled ponytail delightfully askew.

"Corinne, *I found it.*"

I could tell she got it now. Saw it in her eyes.

"Oh Dar," she said and pulled me into her arms. "You beautiful, brilliant lunatic, you. We are going to go to space, aren't we?"

The second person I told was Zilla. Well, I messaged him a graphic of a dancing spaceman and a telescope. I figured he'd get it.

The third person I told was Professor Bellini, my lifelong mentor, luminary, and teacher.

The Lyceum, intent on hiring the brightest minds from around the world to teach the smartest kids ever born, didn't wait too long before recruiting the man responsible for one of the most significant astronomical discoveries of the century. And though I resented any accusations of being a teacher's pet, it must be said that Professor Bellini "call me Sandro" did spend a lot of extra time with me, especially once I declared my focus to be astronomy.

A genuinely remarkable man whose modesty would often lead him to distance himself from his discovery, declaring it a thing of pure chance as opposed to the product of decades of research, Sandro remained one of the smartest normis I have ever met. Also genuinely charismatic, generous, and surprisingly funny. No one expects much humor out of academics, but Bellini told outrageous jokes and took full advantage of the fact that he shared his name with a famous cocktail. "Prosecco and peach nectar together are all the science you need," he'd joke. "A perfect equation."

I was never much of a drinker. But I enjoyed it occasionally; at least it never made me paranoid like Ton's stash. I never missed the alcohol when I didn't have it, though we did bring the bottles of Prosecco and peach nectar with us, courtesy of Sandro. He told us to drink a toast when we've landed and are standing on the surface. This defied numerous laws of exoplanetary physics, of course, but as they say, it's the thought that counts.

He couldn't come with us on this voyage, his age alone would have prohibited it. But he's been with us in spirit; with us as we travel through the galaxy he discovered, his tribute, a new world named for a lost one.

It was strangely, perfectly appropriate that a planet I found lies within the Venezia Del Mare Galaxy. Or spins, is more apt, I suppose. Hidden behind another, larger, planet with an irregular orbit, it was obscured just enough to make it a mystery. My calculations led me to expect it to be there as the wizard behind the curtain, pulling the gravitational strings, affecting celestial bodies around it. And then I found it. There it was.

"There you are," I remember whispering reverently.

"You know in that metaphor *we* are the flying monkeys," Zilla joked when I told him about it.

I nodded. "I'm okay with that."

"Yeah, monkeys are awesome," Ollie added enthusiastically.

And here we are, flying monkeys, all of us, on the way to the mystery planet of our dreams.

We were going to call our ship The Flying Monkeys. Did you know that, Genie?

"I wasn't aware of it, Dar. Thank you for telling me."

It wouldn't have worked, the powers that be, the ones whose bottomless pockets were making it all work, wanted a more proper name. Something Latin, something appropriate to the Lyceum-level geniuses.

We settled on the Lux. It's from my book title, *Post Tenebra Lux*. Through Darkness Light.

More Latin, but it isn't a mere affectation. According to Corinne, from the historical and linguistic perspectives, it's the most perfect widely used language on Earth.

I wasn't sure about writing the book, but we needed to raise awareness. Astronomical news alone all too often goes unnoticed in the world, and this needed notice. There was a lot of publicity. More than I was comfortable with. Zilla was brilliant at it. Even Ton cleaned up nicely to espouse very thoughtful opinions on televised appearances across the globe, though we all knew he was high the entire time.

The book was released the year of both Hurricane Shiva and the latest asteroid near miss. You couldn't have created a more morbidly perfect backdrop if you tried. People were scared enough to explore alternative options. We offered a dazzling one.

A potentially colonizable planet in outer space. A chance for a fresh start among the distant stars. It was a beautiful and easily marketable dream. My book sold well. People were beginning to pay attention. Not a majority by any means—historically speaking, it's been much too long since any majority got behind any smart idea—but enough to fund the project. Enough to get us on our way.

"I am naming it after you," I told Corinne back then, on that perfect morning.

"Absolutely not," she protested in a tone that made me rethink bringing up that it was once her suggestion. "It has to be you. It's your discovery. Plus, Dar is a perfectly good name for a planet."

"I don't know, it might be too short".

"You can always pick a name out of either Greek or Roman mythology. It's been the done thing for ages."

"Not this one." I shook my head. "I want this to be ours. Please let me."

And she did. Though some proclaimed the resulting moniker clumsy and strange and certainly untraditional, it was my choice.

The planet is coming into view just now. It's everything I ever imagined. It is so much more than I ever imagined. It is also visible slightly ahead of our predictions. I must wake the others. But first, one more look. Our Cordar. My Cordar.

DARYL

After Hawaii was destroyed by the lethal combo of devastating earthquakes and rising waters, they stopped building space observatories on the islands altogether. From now on, it was only mainland, as far inland as possible.

For my birthday, Sonya is taking me to the one in Ohio. The telescope there, designed by one of the Chosen, has a resolution high enough to allow me a glimpse at Venezia Del Mare. And maybe, just maybe, at Cordar.

I found out that my son went by Dar a long time ago. Just overheard it one day. But I also couldn't help but notice how assiduously all the other kids and especially him were trying to hide it from me. I found it surprisingly touching, such a sincerely considerate gesture from my boy, who occasionally was prone to not so much disregarding as merely not realizing the feelings of others.

I actually quite liked the sound of Dar. It had a nice ring to it. Sonya told me in her native language it meant *a gift*. "Well, he is that," I told her.

Now we're standing in the grand observatory. It is designed to look like a UFO. I presume this is intentional since a wing of it serves as SETI headquarters. It's more of a SETI 2.0, really. The original institute was all but abandoned in the 2030s, embattled in controversies, marred by persistent failure to engage sufficient public interest and support.

To hear my son tell it, "People have not merely stopped considering the Fermi's Paradox, they stopped even knowing what it was."

The institute was revived by several of the Chosen in recent decades, but thus far, there has been nothing but radio silence for all the loyal Fermi disciples. Whoever's out there isn't talking to us.

Zilla often said that it's probably for the best. According to him, any civilization advanced enough to contact us would be advanced enough to destroy us.

It's a pessimistic perspective, but when I look at what our world has become, I don't know if I can rightly blame anyone for thinking that this grand experiment of humanity, of civilization, might have been a mistake.

When I share these thoughts with Sonya, she listens but disagrees. Somehow, despite all she's been through, she remains remarkably optimistic.

She thinks Daryl and the crew of the Lux will find Cordar habitable, she believes in the future. And I so desperately want to do the same. Even when I lie awake at night, unable to relax enough to fall asleep, with about a million worries racing through my mind.

They've thought of everything—they had to have. They are the smartest people in the world. Their ship alone is the most sophisticated piece of technology ever built. Daryl and his crew gave me a rare tour when the Lux was nearing completion.

It was sleeker than I imagined, perfectly streamlined. I knew the exact terminology wouldn't stick, but the basics are these: the ship's outer shell has been optimized for maximum space radiation protection. There's the main hub area where artificial gravity can be turned on, but mostly it's zero-G and free-floating between the various compartments and personal quarters.

The water is recycled, the air is recycled. Everything that can be recycled is.

The navigation system is the most advanced of any craft ever designed. Between Sam, a somewhat taciturn genius mechanic so quiet I wasn't sure he spoke until I heard his very occasional one-word interjections, and Yoshi, the brilliant programmer and the original designer of the first ever quantum computing platform, the Lux is the pinnacle of technological advancements come to life. To see it was to believe it.

Zilla spent a long time explaining the antimatter/matter powering system to me, though admittedly some of that time was taken up by his numerous pop culture digressions. The kid knows his media.

I was especially a fan of the 3D printers they have on board for food and other needs. They printed me a sample menu, it was lovely. Sometimes you just gotta stand back, shake your head, and marvel at where you are and what you're doing. Printed food. *Tasty* printed food. It's the small things that often get to you.

When Daryl explained to me their traveling/sleeping schedules, I was initially taken aback by the fact that he planned to stay awake longer than anyone and often by himself. But I get it now. I'm looking through this telescope at the galaxy that has existed in our collective minds only for my son's lifetime, and I think how beautiful it is, how majestic it is. Who'd want to sleep through this? Through any minute of it?

I always look for Cordar when I'm looking up. It isn't always easily visible due to the irregular orbit of its neighbor. But I imagine I see it. It's there.

The spectrographic abilities of the modern telescopes are miles ahead of what they used to be but determining the color of distant exoplanets is still no easy task.

We've long thought of Earth as blue, the famous Pale Blue Dot. But from hundreds of light-years away,

Earth looks different too. And it would look even more different and strange under a blue or a red sun.

In theory, and it's all theory for now, Cordar isn't as hot as Earth, but it is more efficient at heating itself because a greater portion of its energy is released as infrared radiation. Its surface is reddish in color, meaning it'll absorb more blue light and therefore more heat. Crucially, there has been some observed vegetation. This, I learned in my classes, can be perceived through the Red Edge effect. Vegetation on Earth, for example, reflects infrared light during photosynthesis, protecting itself against overheating.

Bottom line: there are many factors going into color as we think of it, but in its coloring, as perceived by human eyes through a powerful telescope, Cordar has a blueish/reddish look to it.

And for all the technical mumbo jumbo I'm babbling to Sonya, who to her credit shows a lot of interest, for all the knowledge I have acquired over the years and more recently and more formally in my classes, the main thing is this: Cordar is the first planet ever discovered to fit all the major criteria for habitation. It isn't perfect, but it has a standard orbit, reasonable gravity, enough hydrogen and oxygen in the atmosphere to make a go of it, and, more importantly, water. Not as readily available or as plentiful as on Earth, but beggars can't be choosers. And Cordar is orbiting its star at enough of a distance to possibly both have water in liquid form and not have it evaporate.

It's a dreamboat of an exoplanet. It really is.

I train the lenses until I think it's in my sights. I imagine my son, how close he is to it, perhaps making his planetfall right now. The Lux's transmissions are delayed, and we won't know what's happened until later.

Not since the moon landing of 1969 has the general population globally watched a space adventure with bated breath like this. The world determined to rip itself apart has finally found a shared dream to unite under.

I scoot over to let Sonya see.

"Is that it?" she whispers.

"I think so."

"It's beautiful."

"I know."

"I can't believe they are out there right now."

"I know," I say, again. It is, indeed, a mindboggling concept.

"Happy Birthday, Daryl," Sonya says, finally peeling away, and kisses me on the cheek.

I feel a warm heavy blanket of a deliciously peaceful sensation wrap itself around me. Is this happiness?

DAR

Is this happiness? How many people get to realize their dreams, actualize their dreams? We, the Chosen few, the privileged few, through a quirk of chemically aggravated genetics, through relentless persistence, though aggressive determination, we stand on the surface of a distant planet that may hold the future of all humanity.

We've just made planetfall. I don't know if I have the words to describe how it felt. The gradual approach, the final touchdown. Our breaths held collectively and released exuberantly at last. I remember the stories my father read to me when I was very young. Books he told me he grew up on about distant worlds and the portals which took you there: twisters and wardrobes and all. Opening the hatch of the ship for the first time felt like that. Like going through a portal into another—magical—world. And yet, it's almost as if I know this place.

These are our first steps, but it is all strangely familiar. We've imagined this, dreamed it, planned it for so long. And here we are, at last.

The gravity here is about a fifth less than it is on Earth. We feel lighter. We are elated.

The sky looks like no sky we've seen before. The ground beneath our feet is reddish, reminiscent of a desert, but we know there is water here to be found. We know that if we were to remove our helmets, we would not die from the lack of air, though it will take a long time for humans to adjust to the hydrogen/oxygen balance of Cordar. Ideally, terraforming would help significantly. This ground can be irrigated and made fertile. This planet can sustain life, all indicators show this.

We will study it in detail. Our team is ready for this task and eager to begin.

We are:

Daryl Olsen, astronomer, I, well, I found this place.

Corinne Bellamy, our linguistic expert. Whatever life we discover, she'll be the one figuring out how to communicate with them.

Edward (Zilla) Lumiere, the man responsible for our ingenious propulsion system. And our solar sail backup. Also, a world-renown classic pop culture expert.

Antonio (Ton) Rado, our cultural anthropology expert. The man who can make sure we don't step on any proverbial toes here.

Oliver Darrow, a brilliant zoologist, exozoologist, exobiologist, and cryptozoologist. What this guy doesn't know about different species isn't worth knowing. In theory and in practice, if there are any toes to step on here, he is the man to figure them out and classify them.

Yoshi Daigo, who designed all of our computing and navigational systems, including the irreplaceable Genie, assistant extraordinaire.

Yumi Daigo, who can fix our minds and bodies, should the need arise.

Alice O'Neal, agriculturalist and terraforming expert. She will be able to tell us exactly where to grow what, how, and when, among other things.

And last but not least, Samuel Ward, our mechanic, technician, and an all-around Mr. Fix-It.

We traveled light, our team is small but precision-assembled to optimally ascertain Cordar's assets and habitability. We, all of us, are thrilled to be here and shall begin exploring immediately.

Stay tuned for our findings. Stay tuned for our adventures. And to everyone on Earth watching this, thank you. We will not let you down.

"Live transmission over and out. Genie, you got all of it?"

"Affirmative, Dar."

"How did I do?"

"Do you wish me to honestly appraise your performance, Dar?"

"*Almost* honestly?"

"You did well, Dar. You maintained the casually upbeat, jocular, friendly demeanor the communication network recommended, and I personally appreciated you mentioning me."

"Did Yoshi mess with your settings again?"

"Yes, Dar. Yoshi is trying to optimize my personality."

"Oh, okay then. Well, please beam down the transmission."

"Will do, Dar."

I stumbled back to the Lux bone tired. Who knew literally living out one's dream would be this much work? The transmission alone, the effort it took to sound nothing like myself. But alas, it's all part of the deal. We are here to represent humankind and humankind wants to be in on the process.

"All Neil Armstrong had to do was deliver one line," I complained to Corinne, while we were both getting out of our spacesuits, which Zilla likes to call spacies. Somehow, Zilla had enough energy for all of us, he was practically bouncing off the walls.

We shared the celebratory bellinis and fondly raised a toast to Sandro. The image was recorded for posterity. And then we were done. Time to relax.

I parked my weary bones next to Ton, who never outwardly exhibited or expanded more energy than the bare minimum.

"You did good, brother," said Ton. "Though it's weird to have everyone think of me as Antonio."

I shrugged. "They wanted full names."

"We are as ever at their mercy," Ton agreed.

"Are we really, though?" Zilla ingested an orange hydration cube. "I mean, now that we're here, we can technically do whatever we like. We don't even have to go back."

"Of course, we have to go back," said Alice. "We can't stay here."

"Well, technically, if our recycling facilities operate as planned, we don't have to be beholden to anyone's schedule but our own."

"There are expectations of us. What will people say? Should we be known as that bunch of selfish privileged kid geniuses having a space adventure instead of the intrepid discoverers looking for the future home of humankind?"

Alice lets Zilla's hypotheticals get to her too easily. Her skin is thin, metaphorically, and prone to turning bright red, physically, when she is riled up.

"Relax, Alice," Ollie piped up. "It's just Zilla being Zilla, playing the devil's advocate. And no, Z, this is in no way an invitation for you to start quoting *The Devil's Advocate*."

Aha, I'm not the only one to endure Zilla's relentless fostering of old media.

"You know what we should watch is *Star Wars*." Zilla shifted gears. "Do a marathon."

"*Spaceballs*," Ton threw in. "Definitely *Spaceballs*."

"I have no idea what you two are on about, and I'm going to get some rest." Yumi departed, as dignified as ever. Her brother Yoshi somehow already slipped away. His uncharacteristically public appearance for the transmission probably fried his circuits. Who knew when we'll see him in person next?

Sam was already lost in some book on his screen. Probably a techjournal or a manual. I never saw him read fiction.

Ollie and Alice moved on to the discussion of exomicrofauna.

Ton dozed off.

I wanted to be alone with Corinne. The only choice was to wait for Zilla to get the hint. Typical of the Chosen, he wasn't the quickest with subtle social cues, especially when his system was flooded with adrenaline.

"You mean all that, right, Dar? All that future of humanity business?"

"Sure." I shrugged.

"But do you really?" he pushed. "Do you really care?"

"Yes, I believe I do."

"But you'd want to come here regardless, though, wouldn't you have?"

"Yes." He knew me too well.

"If saving humanity isn't our purpose, then we are indeed just out having a space adventure on everyone's dime," Corinne interjected. "We do have obligations here." Her sense of civic duty was always stronger than either Zilla's or mine.

Zilla shrugged. "They paid for the show, we gave them a show. They paid for hope, we gave them hope."

"That's rather callous."

"You both know as well as I do that once colonized, Cordar would be destroyed. It's what they do, it's what they've always done."

"That's true." Sometime during this conversation Ton woke up. "Empirical evidence throughout history bears Zilla out."

"And here I thought he was just going to use the *Avatar* series as an example," I tried for levity.

"I'm just saying it's so beautiful here, so peaceful. It was an abstract before, but now that we're here, I'd hate to hand it over and watch it be destroyed. We can go back, falsify the test results, say it simply wasn't right after all. They'll be disappointed, but then they'll get back to their meaningless pursuits and forget all about it."

As strange as it was to talk about people back on Earth in terms of us and them, it felt undeniably logical, reasonable. We have always been different, and now those difference were strikingly highlighted by the sheer physical distance. Seen from afar, humanity left a lot to be desired. But then, it was our home. Our families were there. Our history.

Zilla's words made all too much sense to me, haunted me that night as I laid awake next to Corinne, who, I knew, disagreed with it vehemently.

"I don't think we have a choice," I told him then.

"We could just stay here and build a perfect world. Just us."

A strangely tempting thought, but not with billions of lives depending on us. We were tasked with bringing them hope. For all their faults, to deny it seemed unthinkable. Unconscionable.

"I think we have to let them try. It's a death sentence otherwise. Besides, we were always meant to save them from themselves."

"Somebody saaaaaaave me," Zilla sang out.

"Oh no." Corinne laughed. "We will tolerate your foolish ideas, but not your singing, never that."

"I have a beautiful singing voice," he replied, mock offended.

"If there were intelligent lifeforms on this planet and they heard what you call singing, they would eject us back into space immediately," she countered.

"What is that song anyway?" asked Ton. He preferred music without words, tonalities, remixed naturesynch. Joked that all his favorite singers were whales.

"A theme song from *Smallville*, an old TV show about the origin story of Superman," Zilla happily explained. He stopped singing but was still humming it, rebelliously.

"Oh, right, because that's what we are." Ton nodded, acknowledging one of Zilla's favorite recurring conversational themes. "Supermen, Superwomen."

"Is that ... those movies where he's a brooding blue eyed musclebound guy with abundant chest hair?" asked Corinne.

"Oh, no, those were no good. You watched the wrong ones. You should watch either the older ones with Christopher Reeve or the newer ones with Art Regan. Snyder never really got the character of Superman right."

"Well, did your Superman ever have any qualms about saving people?" I asked Zilla.

"Mostly no," Zilla admitted. "He was brought up with good old Kansan values. Kansan? Kansanian? Kansasian?"

"It's Kansan," Corrine specified. "And are you saying we don't have good values?"

"No, we definitely do. It's just that we are too smart for optimism. We may not be supercharged by the power of the yellow sun, but we are superpowered by our minds. We *can* know the future."

"No one can know the future, Zilla," said Corinne, "Not with any certainty."

If only she knew how right she was.

"And with that, as devastated as we are to end this stimulating conversation, we must go to bed," I said, getting up and extending my hand to her.

"He wasn't always sarcastic, you know." Zilla pouted playfully in Corinne's direction. "This is all your doing."

"I can live with that," she tossed back at him and took my hand.

Now we are in bed, she is sleeping soundly, and I am turning the conversation over and over in my head as I am recording it. This will be a private log, Genie. Not ever for public use.

"Noted, Dar."

DARYL

I'm standing in front of my fireplace, looking at all the pictures I have arranged there. It's been made fun of before. I know it's old-fashioned, but it brings me great comfort, and so time after time, I have arranged to have the images of people and places I love printed and framed. They are static as opposed to the more sophisticated dynamic images, meaning they only speak or animate in my mind, in my memory. And I prefer it that way.

I look at the ones of me and my son, arranged roughly chronologically. You can easily observe his growth, by eighteen he overtook my six-foot frame by a good two inches. We look alike, it's often been noted. Our Scandinavian heritage demonstrates itself in both of our appearances: our height, broad shoulders, and sandy blond hair. Only where I'm beginning to stoop and grey, Daryl remains in his prime. My beautiful boy. My brilliant boy.

He's smiling in that one picture, and my memory easily takes me back to the moment. It was right after his book got published. Corinne was there, too, she screengrabbed the image and had it printed and framed for Christmas for me that year.

There are now images of Sonya and me on my mantel, too, but not so many. She is photogenic but camera shy. She's told me of some indigenous peoples' beliefs that taking their picture steals some of their souls. Something like that. Not that it's what she believes. She has, I know, a large box of pictures from her life before, family photos, happy smiling faces all around, and she knows more than most how those images can lie.

I think about it often. Think about how difficult it is to really know and trust someone, to love them unreservedly and completely.

I think about how fortunate I've been in my life to get a chance to do it twice. To have two incredibly special people in my life. I think about how far apart those encounters were in time.

Daryl came into my life so early. An unexpected gift I was nowhere near prepared for. And Sonya came into my life so late I had all but given up hope.

It just goes to show, you really never know. There's no set timeline for these things. Space travel is like that in a way. You can have a blueprint, a planned-out schedule, but overall, there are just too many variables.

Which is what I tell myself, over and over again. How I rationalize not having heard from my son in days now. There are a million reasons for this interruption in transmission, from technical difficulties to solar winds. And yet I lie awake at night imagining infinitely more sinister scenarios. Sonya calls me her great *worrior*, but she understands more than most, more than anyone, what it's like not to know what's going on with your kid.

We were both so proud watching the planetfall transmission. How happy Daryl and his friends looked. The confidence in his voice.

"Neil Armstrong's got nothing on my son," I told Sonya, smiling, and she returned my smile, pride by proxy, proud for me, proud with me.

Now I just need to know he's okay. I am waiting to hear he is okay. I am waiting for a word from the unfathomably far reaches of the universe. I look up to the stars and ask for their benevolence for the intrepid voyagers among them. I'm worried and frightened but I have faith.

DAR

"Genie, switching to real-time experiential narration mode."

"You got it, Dar."

Our first Cordar research expedition is an unqualified success. Ollie and Alice get plenty of samples to study. There is life here, we know that much, but it's difficult to speak to the extent of the biodiversity just yet. We shall have to check out the different and more distant corners of the planet first.

The original design of the Lux included a planetary landing vehicle. That was to allow the Lux to permanently stay put above Cordar, and we'd shuttle back and forth to it. There's sound logic behind a design like that—it allows for the eventual easy departure back to Earth without having to struggle with Cordar's natural gravitational pull.

But a lander is a heavy thing to drag around, and so Zilla and some of his colleagues came up with a thruster system so powerful it all but ensured we'd have no problems taking off when we wanted to. That is why the Lux is actually *parked*, as Zilla jokes, on Cordar. The extra weight, some of it anyway, is instead taken up by the solar sails, a worthy backup for any occasion.

We do have a PEV, our planetary exploration vehicle. Someone on Zilla's team, though he swears it was Sam, made all its surface panels red, so now there's no real choice but to refer to it as the Red Rover. If Sam was indeed responsible, this would be the first sign of a sense of humor hiding somewhere within that quiet man.

The Red Rover shares its artificial intelligence with the main ship, meaning Genie is ever-present here, too. She is our guide, driver, and navigator, all in one.

All we have to do is look around. All we have to do is find signs of life.

Alice comes by some very promising algae. Ollie locates something that might be hoofprints and gets buoyantly excited about the possibility of native ungulates.

And then there are these ... trees, I suppose we can call them that. Not at all like trees back on Earth. Nothing lush like the jungles of Amazon before they began disappearing or collapsing into savannas. Nowhere near the mighty and proud Redwood giants, before the West Coast fires turned them to ash. Not even like a regular forest or a national park kind of tree. No, these look like childhood drawings of trees. Gnarled, malformed, sparse.

Alice is excited about it, though. These trees such as they are, to her, are still a terrific indicator. "A major sign of life," she exclaims happily. "Soil fertility. Means there's a source of water, means there are some proper working chemicals beneath this red dust. For trees to develop like this, they had to have been nourished."

"So, what happened to them, then?" Ollie wonders aloud.

"That I'll have to figure out," she replies, collecting samples.

The most exciting thing that happens to Ollie on our venture is finding some krill in a very shallow basin of water in something like a cave we come across on our third and last hour out. The body of water is barely more than a puddle, and the organisms he finds are, of course, not krill as we know it, but he says that without studying them first, it is as close of a descriptor as he can provide.

Both of these events are very promising. We return to share them with the rest of the crew.

"Oh." Zilla laughs. "you brought us seafood."

I don't know if any of us have even had real seafood. Toxic algae had poisoned the oceans too thoroughly by the time we came around. Our diet, like the diets of many first-world people, has been strictly plant-based for the entirety of our lives.

I wonder if the algae Alice found is toxic. It has a strange greenish-yellow hue to it.

We gather in our spaceship otium, turn on artificial gravity, and make a posterity report of our day for all the people back home.

Then we eat and discuss potential exploration sites for tomorrow. Talk through logistics. Speculate about possibilities, though this is mostly Ton.

"You know, if there is life here, we must be prepared for the fact that it might be hostile," he pontificates upon ingesting an edible.

There were restrictions on the amount of possessions we could bring with us on the Lux, for obvious reasons. I have a pretty good idea what Ton used most of his weight allotment on.

But he makes an excellent point. Something we've never really discussed at length.

"I'm pretty sure I can kick that krill's butt if it comes to it," says Zilla.

Everyone laughs, but the thought has been planted.

The next day brings more fun in the Cordar sun as Ollie puts it. He's in a great mood. I don't know if he slept a wink, but he's made some progress with his krill, and he's high on fumes of discovery.

"I've tested it extensively, and its closest biological mate on Earth would probably be a tardigrade," he tells us.

No wonder he is so excited. Tardigrade is practically Ollie's spirit animal. He has a permaprint of one on his forearm. Ollie's the only tattooed person I know. He says it is to honor his Native ancestors. Though his surfer looks may not reflect it, he traces the maternal side of his heritage to the First Nation peoples of Canada.

"Tardigrades can tolerate the most extreme conditions, so this isn't necessarily the most auspicious of finds in certain respects," he says. "We want something more conditional, more fragile even, to show that life here can be endured by creatures other than the extreme survivors. But in the grand scheme of things, this is still exceptionally promising."

"You know, I had hoped for megafauna, originally," says Alice. "I don't know why. And, of course, I knew the odds were stacked against it. But there's something about discovering a wild and lush world like that ..." She drifts off, a dreamy look in her eyes.

"I think you've watched too many of those dinosaur movies with Zilla," Corinne suggests jokingly.

"I think we all have," I agree.

"They didn't even get the name right on that franchise," Ollie chimes in. "It should have been

Cretaceous Park. Most of those dinosaurs were from the Cretaceous period."

"Zilla would call you a pedant right now." Corrine grins.

"But I'm right."

"Doesn't have the same ring to it, though," says Corinne.

"There we go, science bowing down to aesthetics."

"Oh, don't pout, you know you love semantics as much as the next person." Corrine hits him in the shoulder playfully.

"You have arrived at your destination, team."

"Thank you, Genie."

Here we go. This location was selected after careful research, based on drone imaging. There seems to be a large concentration of activity here, more of those strange trees, something very closely resembling a stream, and some new caves to explore.

We set off, full of hope. Red dust under our feet. The strange Cordar gravity making us feel lighter than we are, putting an artificial bounce in our step.

Over time this gravity, if unaltered, would exact a toll on a human body. There would be some loss of muscle and bone mass, and a change in calcium levels.

Future Cordar colonists might be taller, with puffier faces and skinnier legs. I imagine something like a cartoon character. I shake the thought off. That future is too far away to worry about right now.

I'm here, in this bewildering, for-so-long-unimaginable present. We are entering a cave—an organic creation by all appearances. There are rock formations here, Cordar's equivalent of stalagmites and stalactites. There's water. Not a lot, but enough to get both Alice and Ollie excited.

I try to relax. Despite having traveled here in a spaceship, the ultimate of all enclosures, I have never been a fan of closed-in spaces. Corinne knows this. She reaches out, takes my hand, and squeezes it reassuringly.

We walk around the cave, hand-in-hand, as if we are on some strange spelunking date. I look at my feet, ensconced in my bulky spaceshoes. How alien they look here.

And then Corinne stops dead in front of one wall.

"Dar," she whispers with something that can only be described as awe or reverence in her voice. "Look."

I look, and I can feel my heart stop and restart itself, the whoosh of a sudden blood rush sounding just like the ocean in my ears.

There are carvings on the wall. Images crafted with deliberation if not skill. It's official.

We are not alone.

DARYL

My son never got into comic books as a kid. Not like I did. Not like any of my friends growing up. But then again, Daryl wasn't like any other kid.

I was always a huge fan, and Superman was always my favorite. I had a box of those old comics just waiting to be passed down and eventually, they were. To Zilla. And boy, was he thrilled.

I remember trying to explain to Daryl the appeal of Superman.

"You see, he can do whatever he wants, he has the power to do whatever he wants, but he always chooses to do the right thing. Because he is a hero."

"And how does he determine what the right thing is?" Daryl inquired.

"He can just tell. He has a strong moral compass."

"And what defines a strong moral compass?" The kid had to have been only five or six at that time.

Already curious about the concepts most adults can't master.

"Having good values. It takes having a good brain and a good heart to know right from wrong."

"It still seems kind of arbitrary," said Daryl, pondering my words. "I can see how it would apply in simple situations, but not the morally complex or ambiguous ones."

I laid off Superman after that.

Interestingly enough, my son did get into comics after all, albeit later in life. Courtesy of the inimitable Zilla and his anachronistic obsessions. Well, maybe not *into it* into it, but at least he developed a sort of ironic appreciation of the format.

Even make a joke about it.

"Dad," he asked me once, "how would Superman solve the trolley problem?"

I was pleased I actually knew what it was—recently taking a back seat in Daryl's philosophy class paid off. It's been around for ages apparently, a system of thought experiments and moral dilemmas about whether it is ever worth it to sacrifice one person for the lives of many.

"I don't know, kiddo. How *would* Superman solve the trolley problem?"

"He'd stop the trolley," said Daryl, smiling proudly.

Of course, he would. I remember my heart overflowing with love for Daryl in that moment.

And now my son is on a mission to save the world. He has, in a way, become a Superman in his own right. Him and his friends.

And I know, though his mind works in unfathomably complex ways when it comes right down to it, he'll make the right choice, every time. I may be a *worrier*, but Daryl is a warrior. Even if he doesn't know it yet.

DAR

"We need to go. We need to go now."

Corinne nods, she is as stunned as I am. My mind is already playing through the implications of our discovery. There are many possible scenarios. None of them are good.

If there was life on Cordar, how could it have gone undetected all this time? We'd sent several exploratory probes ahead of our arrival. The planet was surveyed extensively, and the data was analyzed by the brightest minds at the Lyceum. I personally supervised it. We missed nothing, I'm sure of it. I *was* sure of it, anyway.

So, what is this? A race of cave dwellers sophisticated enough to avoid all detection by advanced technology? What are the odds?

We grab Alice and Ollie, book it to the Red Rover, and take off in a cloud of orangish dust.

We tell them about the images while on the move. They are as stunned, as incredulous as we are. Though still rather more intrigued than alarmed.

"There could be a rational explanation," Ollie starts. "The images might be old. From bygone peoples. Like the cave art on Earth."

"It's possible," says Corinne. "The quality of rock makes it difficult to estimate the age without formal tests. But there was something about it. Something like ... a modern sensibility. Not artistic sophistication per se, but something that suggested ..." She pauses, looking for the best way to describe it.

"Something that suggested Earth-style graffiti," I finish.

"Exactly." She snaps her fingers. "Like street art."

"So, you think...?"

I don't let Alice finish. She can tell me I'm wrong and overreacting later. "I think we need to get back to the Lux immediately."

We arrive quickly. Genie takes us as fast as Red Rover can go. I can tell something's wrong before we even enter the ship.

"Are those footprints?"

There are shapes in the sand and dust. They certainly do look like footprints.

The Lux's portal shows signs of damage. We enter and the damage becomes obvious. The main power is out. The secondary one has kicked in, but the atmosphere is distinctly dimmer.

"You're okay. You're okay." Ton drapes himself over me and Corinne. "I was so worried. We were so worried."

"What happened?"

"We were attacked, man. Out of nowhere. They rushed in, did a quick smash and grab. Mostly foods from what I can tell. It was over so quickly."

"Is everyone alright?"

"They knocked out Yumi. I think she has a concussion She thinks she has a concussion. She's resting. Yoshi and Zilla and Sam are working to restore power, assess the damage, and stabilize the systems."

"What were they like? The attackers?"

"Not the first close encounter I was hoping for," says Ton, rubbing his forehead. "I couldn't even tell you, really. I mean, they threw in something like a smoke bomb. There was a lot of smoke. They were humanoid, I know that much. Their clothing was baggy, obscuring, like camo. I didn't hear speech, but they were definitely coordinated. This was a planned attack."

We lock down. We sit and wait for Zilla, Yoshi, and Sam to tell us just how extensive of a hit we took. Alice and Ollie go to take stock of our rummaged through supplies. We don't actually have a lot of food stock, most of what we ingest is 3D printed. There are just some things, the *inimitables* as we call them: Zilla's coffee, Corinne's chocolates, Ollie's mother's jams.

Things like that. I brought a box of muffins with me on board. Terribly impractical and short-lived pleasures, I know, but absolutely worth it.

All those treats are gone now. So are some printable cartridges, though not the printer itself. The machine is simply too massive.

"They tried to take it," says Ton, "but couldn't."

In an emergency takeover protocol, Genie is authorized to lock down the crew and release a fast-acting toxin neutralizer into the air. Even if the crew cannot be securely locked down, they can quickly be administered an antidote. It's what saved us all. According to Ton, the attackers were affected by it, stumbling out with half the energy of their initial onslaught.

Eventually, they emerge, our warriors. Well, Zilla and Sam do. Yoshi is with Yumi and won't leave her side.

"It's less serious than you might be thinking," says Zilla, his face grey with exhaustion. "Primarily it's the comm panel that took the hit. No messages home for a while. But all fully reparable. Because some geniuses—" He rolls his eyes self-deprecatingly but not without pride, "—created such a fortress of a system to begin with."

"Ship took a beating." Sam sighs. "I can repair most of it easily enough with time, but we may need to re-up some basic security. I'm reinforcing the portal."

That's probably as many words as Sam can say at once. Certainly, as many as I've ever heard him say at once. The situation must be serious indeed.

"We need to have a team meet ASAP," I say. "This changes..."

"Everyfreakingthing," Zilla finishes.

Yumi looks alright, there's a bandage on her head and Zilla took to calling her Rambo, though I don't think she gets the reference. Yoshi seems uncomfortable, like he's dying to be back in his private enclosed safe space.

We are huddled together in the otium. Gravity's off. We're floating in an effort to conserve energy.

"Sam should be here shortly," says Ton. "He's just finishing with the portal."

"So, opinions, thoughts, ideas?" I start.

We were never short on those. We discuss this for a while, batting back and forth every possibility from scientific to fictional, but there are simply too many unknowns.

Based on what we do know, there is a reasonably advanced species here. They are humanoid in appearance and are comfortable with violence and theft. And why wouldn't they be if they perceive us as the invaders? Even if they don't know humanity's shoddy track record with colonization.

It seems our options are as follows:

1. We can leave. This would be a devastating failure for all of us involved with the project, for humankind in general. But it would be a peaceful and easy resolution.

2. We can stay. Try to locate the locals. Try communicating with them. See if we can work together.

3. We can continue our research, albeit while taking every precaution, and see if we can establish a nonthreatening presence, and hope they'll eventually feel comfortable enough to approach us. Ideally, in a more peaceful manner.

No one supports option one, except Yoshi, who appears to have had enough adventure and is worried about his sister. If we're honest with ourselves, we the Chosen are much too cerebral, brainforward, intellectually curious, to walk away from a puzzle this great. Option one appears to have been postulated for posterity only. After the initial reactions of unwelcome surprise and fear wear off, we know we're not going anywhere.

Number two is a much more popular option. Corinne loves the idea of opening communication. This would be the pinnacle of all her training, a dream come true.

"Zilla made me watch *The Arrival* three times. I am more than ready," she jokes.

"I'm noting for posterity, this is the 2016 movie of that name," adds Zilla. "And I did also steam you the original Ted Chiang's short story to read."

"Yes. See, ready."

Option three is a favorite of Ollie and Alice. As frightened as they were originally, now that the shock has worn off, they are back to being the ultimate dispassionate scientists with the greatest intergalactic discoveries at their fingertips.

"So, what do we do? We vote?" I suggest.

Funny how no matter how much you can prepare for something, life can still throw sticks in your spokes. Funnier still that I remember that expression now, after all these years. It's something my dad used to say.

We did originally discuss the possibility of there being intelligent life on Cordar. Of course, we did. But scan after scan, drone data coverage after drone data coverage, had convinced us of it being too distant of a prospect, and we shifted our focus to other, more practical matters. If only we knew.

"Yes, I think vote we must," says Zilla.

And so, we agree to sleep on it and decide in the morning with fresh heads, though how well we'll sleep after the day we've had is anyone's guess.

The following morning the mood is somber as we ingest our breakfast nutricubes in pensive silence.

Sam walks in. "Something you should see before you vote."

We follow him out to the portal. He hits the button that turns the top section of it transparent so that we can see outside.

There's a motley crew of individuals out there, standing together; their appearance obscured by their clothing which seems to be a mix of spacesuit gear and rags, and there's a message, scrawled into the dirt in front of them, but clear and legible. It says:

We need to talk.

This changes things. Again. Drastically.

If nothing else, it obviates the need for the vote, at least the immediate need. The answer has been brought to us, in a way, but do we dare go outside to hear it?

"They've attacked us. They proved to be violent. We can't just go out there," says Alice, sensibly.

"We can communicate through written messages," Corinne suggests. "We already know they understand English."

"That might be for the best," we all concede—a safe, if cowardly, solution.

We agree on a text and then have Genie project it outward toward our visitors.

"We come from Earth. We mean you no harm. We only wish to visit and study your planet. We are nonviolent. Our goals are scientific in nature. We wish to communicate with you, but we are concerned about further violence."

"If only we could put a number on how many devastating colonizations started off with peace professing messages," Ton muses.

Zilla elbows him, and they share an *Avatar* series-based inside joke.

It doesn't do much to lift the tension that has enveloped all of us in its steel grasp.

We wait as our visitors discuss our words.

Then, in an elaborate display, they slowly take out and throw down their weapons: a fairly primitive range of spears, bows and arrows, bone knives. Entirely too unsophisticated for people wearing remnants of spacesuits.

They gesture at the discarded arsenal at their feet, then hold up their arms to show them empty, and make a beckoning gesture to us.

No words are necessary. They are making a concession. We must assent, mustn't we?

"Not all of us," says Yumi, up and about, but still seemingly weak, or maybe it's just the aftermath of the recent violence echoing through.

We agree on me, Zilla, Ton, and Corinne. I'm dead against Corinne going but have no way of asserting my will with her without pulling rank.

This seems like the sort of situation to make a wreck of the gender politic notion of the last century. Is this a display of toxic masculinity that I should want to leave my woman behind in safety? For posterity, let it be said, that the decision is primarily practical.

Expandable personnel first. Yumi's injured, Yoshi and Sam are too essential to the mission. Alice and Ollie have samples that may revolutionize exoplanet studies. Zilla really should be staying behind too, but he won't. Nothing and no one can make him.

Corinne and Ton, in theory, can advise on the subtleties of communication, from both linguistic and cultural perspectives. But something tells me we might not be needing that.

We emerge from the portal. There's trepidation in our step that we're trying to hide. This is the exact opposite of how it felt at first to set foot on Cordar's soil. Was it only days ago? It seems impossible.

We approach the group, get to within a conversing distance, all too weary of the cache of weapons between us.

"Hello," I say and lift my hand in greeting, palm facing them, open.

One of them—their leader?—steps forward.

"Hello," he says, mimicking my hand. "Hello, Dar."

My first instinct, I'm ashamed to say, is to turn tail and sprint back to the ship. A sort of primordial fear guiding the reptilian regions of the cerebellum. How does this person know my name? I'm just barely now wrapping my head around the fact that he exists and speaks English. How many surprises does this planet hold for me?

Corinne squeezes my hand and even through the thick protective glove of my suit I feel her reassurance. It's all it takes. I refocus.

I am a scientist. I am a genius. I have a brain optimized for observing and processing information, so that's what I do.

I observe before me a group of individuals who have seen better times. They are human, I can see now, not just humanoid. Human, but deformed. There is a man with a single eye centrally positioned in the middle of his head like the mythical Cyclops. There's a man with three legs, the third limb, vestigial and awkward, withering at his side. There's a woman with only one arm, though I can't tell if that's due to a deformity or injury. They all have terrible greenish-yellowish complexion, bloodless lips, sallow skin, thin hair. Their eyes are sunken. Their features, their very bones are peculiarly etiolated as if they were plants desperately reaching out for the warmth and light of an unfriendly sun.

They are definitely wearing spacesuits, remnants of spacesuits to be precise. Some have helmets, but not the rest, some only have torso sections or leg protectors. The rest is patched together with an assortment of all-purpose synthetic fabrics, something you'd find used for upholstery or storage on a ship, certainly nothing that can offer adequate protection from the elements.

They look tired, desperate, and, most of all, hungry. Not the passive kind of curl-in-a-corner-and-dream-of-bread-crusts hunger, but an active maddening driving force. If I had to guess, I'd say it's their main motivation for everything: for them being here now, for their attack, for all that's to come. People that hungry are dangerous. Back on Earth, Africa is on fire with hunger wars. Here, we can't afford to start or stoke that kind of fire.

Their leader is dressed in the most complete spacesuit out of all of them. His helmet's face shield is damaged, making his face difficult to see. He seems to realize it and takes it off. Shakes his dirty longish hair out of his eyes. I recognize his features. Of course, I do.

"Hello, Mal."

Malcolm Armstrong IV. The only Chosen ever expelled from the Lyceum. Well, he's certainly come a long way since.

And there, by his side, his righthand man. I recognize him now, too. It's Brent. So that's what became of him. He looks thirty pounds lighter and thirty years older than the last time I saw him. But he's smirking still, that same arrogant smirk.

"Long time no see," Mal says, amiably.

"Indeed." I nod politely, cautiously.

"I've been expecting you," he proceeds. "We," he gestures around him, "have been expecting you."

"And here I am."

"And here you are."

"Been waiting long?"

"Too long," he says, and beneath the glib jocularity of his tone, I hear the note of bitter truth. And somehow, I know then *that's* what happened. That's why they look like this. There has been some kind of a terrible miscalculation somewhere down the line. They have been waiting for far too long. Stranded here with insufficient provisions, struggling to survive.

"These are my friends," Mal continues, quickly recovering his composure. "You all probably know them as the Shunned."

Oh, Mal, you've gone and done it, brought the Shunned to space, a place that seems to find them as unwanted as their home planet did.

"You attacked us," I say mildly.

"That was wrong of us." He nods. "I apologize. We just got... overexcited."

I stand there quietly, waiting for more.

"We have made some ... planning errors and now find ourselves rather desperate needing some supplies. We shouldn't have done what we did, and it won't happen again. We were hoping we could negotiate. Maybe some sort of an exchange. We provide you with information about this place, you print us some food."

His tone is light, but I can hear desperation there. This isn't really a negotiation; he will not take no for an answer. There's too much at stake for him.

"How are you here, Malcolm?" asks Ton. The million-dollar question, the one we've all been dying to ask.

"Same way you are." Mal curls his lips into a nasty smile. "A spaceship brought us."

"When did you arrive?"

"It feels like a lifetime ago. Time doesn't pass the same way here."

"There was no information on Cordar until I discovered it. No technology available prior to the Lux's proprietary plans for a trip like this."

"Exactly," says Mal. And for a second, he lets his evil side shine. It's there in his eyes, ever so briefly, and then it's gone. "Thanks, Daryl. Thanks, Zilla."

Well, at least now I know I wasn't being paranoid, Ton's product was never to blame, my data *was* hacked and stolen back in school. I am looking at the party responsible for it.

And now I remember there was that time Zilla echoed my paranoia back at me. I look at him now, and I know he's thinking the same thing. I see the fury in his eyes.

"It was incomplete, of course. You must have found out, bumped up your firewalls. Our guys are good, but we couldn't compete with Yoshi. We did our best, though. Built our best. My money, Brent's money, came in handy."

"And you launched without anyone noticing?" asks Zilla, incredulously.

"Oh, wait. You mean, you don't remember the famous rocket launch site explosion in the news some time ago?"

"In Canada," whispers Corinne.

"That's right, Nunavut. Turns out with enough money you can hush up just about anything, especially when every single item on the news is some kind of a disaster".

"That was years ago".

"Yes, it was. We should have been more established by now, but there have been ... problems. Our entry into the planetary atmosphere hadn't gone smoothly, our 3D printer didn't survive, and now we just need some help. You will help, won't you? We are, after all, your fellow space travelers, your fellow geniuses."

"We need to think about it, discuss it with our crew," I say, playing for time.

"Sure, sure." Mal nods, as if he's disappointed but was expecting something like this. "Talk it over with your people. We'll be back tomorrow, around the same time for your answer. Oh, and Daryl, it's good to see you."

I have never punched someone in my life. Never laid a hand on anyone in anger. But I feel my fingers close into a fist as I force myself to smile back at Mal and promise to see him tomorrow. They wait for us to retreat to our ship, then pick up their weapons, and leave.

We head straight into the otium. We have much to discuss.

It is strange, this balance of hostility and civility we seem to have established with Mal and his people. They let us go have a discussion in peace, and cautious as we are, we do not fear an outright attack while we do. It's almost as if they want this done a certain way. Recognition, legitimacy. In a way, hasn't it always been what they wanted? Before everything that's happened, and all the things that have gone wrong.

They seem to trust us or understand us enough to know we will not leave. Our mission remains our primary objective. This planet is too important. The question is: can it be shared? On Earth, people have historically made nothing but a mess of any and all attempts to share. But this is a brave new world. Do the rules change? Do we? What kind of people do we want to be here in a place that could be our future home? What kind of people do we need to be to survive?

We talk for hours, but the bottom line never shifts. We cannot share our much needed and precision budgeted supplies with Mal and the Shunned. They are thieves, liars, cheats. They are violent. They will never stop taking, and nothing we'll give them will ever be enough.

Had they asked in the first place, came to us and asked, instead of attacking the Lux, their request would have merited more consideration. As things stand, they have proven themselves to be unworthy of our help.

While we parleyed, Alice and Ollie made some breakthroughs. It turns out the krill has potential for sentience and algae for a food source, albeit not without side effects.

"It has proteins, but not the kind our bodies are able to process correctly," says Alice. And yet it is obvious that Mal and his people have been surviving on algae.

"It explains the color. You are what you eat and all that."

"Like the flamingos," piped in Ollie.

"So, they are starving to death and slowly poisoning themselves with local offerings," Zilla sums up. "Serves them right."

I can tell he's still mad about the theft of his ideas. He has always been devoutly zealous about intellectual property.

"Remember *Gattaca*?" he asks. "That old science fiction movie with two brothers, one, Anton is genetically enhanced, the other, Vincent, isn't."

"Um ... vaguely."

"Well, in it," Zilla proceeds, undeterred, "Anton and Vincent reminisce about going for a long-distance swim. Somehow, despite being genetically inferior, Vincent would kick Anton's butt. And when Anton asks how he did it, Vincent says he never saved any energy for the swim back."

"Okay and this story is in service of ...?" says Alice impatiently. She never really got into Zilla's old media obsession.

"That's what Mal and his people did," explains Zilla. "They gave it a crazy push, saving nothing for the trip back because they were likely never planning to go back. Why would they? Earth was dying. People there hated the Shunned at the best of times. They probably figured this would be a fresh start. They just miscalculated."

"That makes perfect sense, actually," Yoshi has emerged from his enclave for this. "That's how they were able to beat us here. They only planned for half of the journey."

Zilla nods grimly. "Sound plan until it wasn't. But their failure isn't our responsibility."

"Does everyone agree with this?" I ask.

Ollie shrugs. "We didn't have much to do with them back home, why start now?"

I wait for Zilla to play his customary role of the devil's advocate, but he remains uncharacteristically quiet.

"They are human like us," I say in his stead, though without much conviction. "They are geniuses like us. They are closer to us in than any living thing on this planet and many back on Earth."

"Did you feel this closeness when you were out there speaking with them?" asks Corinne.

"No." I shake my head, honestly. "I did not."

"It's never going to be as simple as giving them some food. They will never be satisfied struggling out there, while we have all that we have. And more importantly—" Zilla dramatically pauses for effect. "—they will never let us leave. Not if we are their only meal ticket. Not if our goal is to bring more people here, people they have done all this just to get away from."

And that seals the deal. We all know Zilla is right. Our great minds do proverbially think alike.

"They'll never take no for an answer." I state the obvious, for posterity's sake.

Everyone nods in tacit agreement. It is understood then.

And we all know what we must do next. We must face up to the terrible inevitability.

I remember the conversation I had with my dad a long time ago, back when he was trying to get me into his beloved Superman comics. I think he struggled with making the appeal relevant to me. He should have used the Shunned. Their circumstances were different, certainly, but people have overcome worse. In theory, they have been given the same intellectual advantages as us. In theory, they could have done a great many things with it. They could have been the ones to save the world. Instead, they chose a different path, made different choices. Did they think they were doing the right thing, too? Did that thought even enter the equation? It all led us here. To this situation, this standoff.

I think the comics have it wrong because they make it look easy and doing the right thing, even knowing what that might be, isn't an easy task. But one has to try.

Tomorrow, when Mal and the Shunned return, they will have their answer. It won't be the answer they were hoping for, but it is the only one we can give them. For the sake of our self-preservation, for the sake of our mission, for the sake of everyone back home.

And when they turn on us in a predictable reaction, we will be ready. Our 3D printer doesn't just print food.

By nature, I believe most of the Chosen are pacifists, but sometimes, it simply isn't enough. We came on this mission as an outstretched hand, but we must now fold our fingers into a fist, and defend what we believe in.

We hope the future won't judge us too harshly. We are doing this so that there can be a future. We are no heroes, but we are trying to do the right thing all the same.

Maybe that's what heroism is: doing the difficult right thing. Or maybe we are just rationalizing murder. It's difficult to say at the moment. But I hope it's the former, *we* hope it's the former.

After it's over, we will return to the normal transmissions schedule. Yoshi assures us by then our coms will be fully restored. I've recorded all of this, but I haven't yet decided whether it should ever be made public. Why tarnish our images? Why tarnish this story?

Ton says every civilization is born awash in blood. It's a birth like any other birth. Still, what a cost to pay.

By birth and by choice, we are the dreamers. The thinkers. The inventors. The adventurers. We didn't ask to be anyone's saviors. We were never meant to kill, but we have evolved once to save a dying world. I know we can do so again.

DARYL

Sonya and I moved in together. It made too much sense not to. I don't want to be away from her, she doesn't want to be away from me. Both of us have had enough alone time to last a lifetime.

Now she is standing in our kitchen, carefully shaping pancakes on the griddle into...

I squint. "Are those space rockets?"

"You bet. Can't have you be the only Daryl Olsen not eating space food."

I hug her from behind and kiss her head. Enjoy the smell of her hair. Enjoy the smell of breakfast cooking.

"Careful," she says, "I don't want to mess up the thrusters."

"No, we definitely can't have messed up thrusters," I agree, moving away in the general direction of the coffeemaker.

"Have you had a cup already, love?" I ask her, pouring myself one.

"No, I'm naturally this bright-eyed and bushy-tailed rocket pancake maker." Sonya smiles. She is fueled by caffeine and has had to cut down due to the imported beans going up in cost.

"I saw the newsfeed on my screen about all those Brazilian droughts. Looks like the coffee is set to become a luxury item."

"At least it won't die out like bananas," I say, taking a sip. I miss bananas dearly. I'd trade coffee for bananas, I think.

"Someday in the near future, we'll have to learn to make do without," she sighs. But until that day …"

"Cheers."

"Cheers."

We toast each other with our coffee mugs. Look at each other with the easy affection of people happy in each other's company.

The newsfeed is droning on in the background.

Sonya flips some pancakes on our plates, sets them on our small kitchen table, squeezes some syrup atop. The sun hits their glistening golden surfaces just right, and for a moment they do indeed look like space rockets.

The newsfeed voice changes.

"We interrupt this broadcast to bring you the long-awaited new transmission from our crew on Cordar …"

AFTERWORD

I very much like the idea of writing as broadly as I read. Despite having some astrophysics classes under my belt, I must say that writing science fiction doesn't come as easily as other genres to me. Which makes this story all the more special.

As always, my main interest is in psychology: the things people do and the reasons behind them. And yes, I am a huge fan of Superman. So, I wanted to write a story about what Supermen and Superwomen might look like in the near future and what they'd be willing to do to save the world. And I dragged them all the way across the universe to find out.

Thank you, dear reader, for tagging along. Writers are nothing without readers, mere scribblers. I am so very grateful you've chosen to take the time to check out my story. I hope you found it interesting and thought-provoking, or at the very least, entertaining. Either way, thank you.

Additional gratitude to the following:

Seb Doubinsky, a brilliant writer and a great friend, for telling me *Arrokoth* deserves a proper publisher *and* introducing me to one.

Nate Ragolia of Spaceboy Books for being that proper publisher. Thank you for loving my story and booking it a ride aboard the Spaceboy Rocket.

Gary and Tyler Sarno, the best real-life father/son team out there.

My awesome BETA readers for feedback and editing suggestions.

All the fantastic authors who took the time to read my story and contribute very generous blurbs.

Atticus Morton for being the best fan an author could ask for and all-around excellence.

The internet for making sure I don't embarrass myself too much.

And most importantly, my beautiful, brilliant wife, Chelsea, for continuous support, encouragement, and inspiration. This and every story I write is first and foremost for her. Always.

ABOUT THE AUTHOR

Mia Dalia is an internationally published author, a lifelong reader, and a longtime reviewer of all things fantastic, thrilling, scary, and strange. Her short fiction has been published by online by Night Terror Novels, 50-word stories, Flash Fiction Magazine, Pyre Magazine, Tales from the Moonlit Path and in print anthologies by Sunbury Press, HellBound Press, Black Ink Fiction, Dragon Roost Press, Unsettling Reads, Moon, Anthology of Lunar Horror, Phobica Books, Psycho Toxin Press, Wandering Wave Press, Bullet Points vol. 3, Critical Blast, and DraculaBeyondStoker Magazine.

Her fiction will be featured in the upcoming anthologies by Nightshade Press, Off-Topic Publishing, Exploding Head Press, Sinister Smile Press, and Crystal Lake Publishing.

Mia's Noir tales have been published by Mystery Magazine and Bang! Noir Anthology from Headshot Press.

Her short fiction has been featured by narrative podcasts such as Zoetic Press' Alphanumeric and Tales to Terrify.

Mia's novelettes, *Smile So Red* , *Spindel*, and *The Trunk*, are available on Amazon.

Mia's novellas, *Tell Me a Story* and *Discordant*, have been published by PsychoToxin Press. The latter comes with its own soundtrack inspired by the story.

Her debut novel, *Estate Sale*, was published in April of 2023 to rave reviews.

She makes her science fiction debut with a novella, *Arrokoth*.

Find her at
➡Official website:https://daliaverse.wixsite.com/author
➡Twitter: @ Dalia_Verse
➡FB: DaliaVerse
➡https://linktr.ee/daliaverse

ABOUT THE PUBLISHING TEAM

Nate Ragolia is a lifelong lover of science fiction and its power to imagine worlds more hopeful and inclusive than the real one. His first book, *There You Feel Free*, was published by 1888's Black Hill Press in 2015. Spaceboy Books reissued it in 2021. He's also the author of *The Retroactivist* (2017). His most recent book, *One Person Can't Make a Difference* (2022), was featured on Tor.com's Can't Miss Indie Press Speculative Fiction list, and was translated into Italian for Ringworld Sci-Fi in 2023. He founded and edited *BONED*, a literary magazine, and also created two webcomics. Nate is also a husband and a dog dad.

Shaunn Grulkowski has been compared to Warren Ellis and Phillip K. Dick and was once described as what a baby conceived by Kurt Vonnegut and Margaret Atwood would turn out to be. He's at least the fifth best Slavic-Latino-American sci-fi writer in the Baltimore metro area. He's the author *Retcontinuum*, and the editor of *A Stalled Ox* and *The Goldfish* for 1888/Black Hill Press.